CARTEL PUBLICATIONS
PRESENTS

# HERSBAND
## MATERIAL
### A NOVEL

BY C. WASH

PUBLISHER'S NOTE:
This book is a work of fiction. Names, characters, businesses,
Organizations, places, events and incidents are the product of the
Author's imagination or are used fictionally. Any resemblance of
Actual persons, living or dead, events, or locales are entirely coin-
cidental.

Library of Congress Control Number: 2013931063
ISBN 10: 0984993061
ISBN 13: 978-0984993062

Cover Design: Davida Baldwin www.oddballdsgn.com
Editor: Advanced Editorial Services
Graphics: Davida Baldwin
www.thecartelpublications.com
First Edition

Printed in the United States of America

# THIS NOVEL IS A PART OF

# THE CARTEL PUBLICATIONS

A SUBSIDIARY OF
## THE CARTEL PUBLICATIONS

# CHECK OUT OTHER TITLES BY
# THE CARTEL PUBLICATIONS

## WWW.THECARTELPUBLICATIONS.COM

# ACKNOWLEDGEMENTS

First off, I want to acknowledge the LGBT community as a whole. It's not easy being who you are despite how society looks at you. No matter what, continue to hold your head up high and be proud of the skin you're in. #equalityinmarriage.

Second, I want to acknowledge *ALL* my family. Thank you for loving me, always. To my Mommy, Big Sheil, thank you for showing me how to work and for raising me strong, I know it wasn't always easy. I love you. To my sister, CeCilia Washington, BKA, CeCe, BKA, Seven, my right hand nigga, although I was jealous when Mommy and Daddy brought you home from the hospital initially, you have grown to be one of my best friends. Continue to live out your dreams, the world and Hollywood needs your talent. I love you. Love you too Angel! To my son, D'Juan Bishop, make sure you find your passion in life. It doesn't matter how long it takes, there is nothing in the world better than finding out what you like to do, then getting paid to do it. Don't worry, you'll find it, I believe in you. I love you! To my other son, Kajel, I'm proud of you for being a man and raising our grandbaby, KJ, with love and dedication. I love you both.

To all the Cartel Publications fans thank you so much for always holding us down. You guys mean the world to us and I hope I do you proud with this one.

Last but not least, to my partner, best friend, boss chick and my baby, Toy, there are no words invented that would completely express my love for you. I would not be the woman, person, or boss I am today if it weren't for you.

Thank you for always believing in me and pushing me to great heights. I hope I make you proud.

I'm not a talker, so I'll wrap here. If I did not mention you, know that it's not personal, I have slow brain but I still love you.

Charisse "C. Wash" Washington
www.thecartelpublications.com
authorcwash@yahoo.com
www.facebook.com/cwashvp
www.twitter.com/cwashvp
instagram publishercwash

What's Good Babies,

As I'm writing this letter for C. Wash's debut novel, I'm reminded of my first novel Rainbow Heart. To tell you the truth I didn't foresee having the success I have now, or the success I will attain later, after I penned that book. I was just writing...with no formal training or plan in mind. When the book was done, it didn't do much in terms of success, but I was overwhelmed with joy. Because I did what so many couldn't...I wrote my first book!

Remembering the old days makes me so proud to be writing this letter for C. Wash, the VP of The Cartel Publications. I am amazed! I am in awe! And I can't stop smiling. She jumped out there and created a stunning debut and I'm proud to stamp this novel with the CP brand fans have come to adore. Writing a book is not easy and it certainly takes guts, talent and dedication. Luckily for us the VP has them all. I think fans will be taken by Mystro and Native, the characters C. Wash created, I know I am!

Keeping in line with tradition, we want to give respect to a trailblazer paving the way. With that said we want to recognize:

*Azarel*

Azarel is the CEO of Life Changing Books. She is also the author of Bruised, Daddy's House, Carbon Copy, and many more. Although she excels as an author and publisher, she is also a solid businesswoman, wife, mother and friend, who we respect and adore.

Well, the time has come to jump into Hersband Material. So grab a glass of your favorite poison, sit back and enjoy.

T. Styles
President & CEO
The Cartel Publications
www.thecartelpublications.com

# DEDICATION

This novel is dedicated to my motivation, my inspiration, my aspiration and true boss bitch, Toy Styles. You believed in me and encouraged me, then led by example and I am eternally grateful for you. By finally dropping my first novel, I can truly understand how hard you work everyday and just how extremely talented you are. I hope I grow up to be one tenth of the author you are now and will become. Thank you, I LOVE YOU!

# PROLOGUE

Mystro Mason stood in the semi-crowded courtroom with a thin layer of perspiration on her forehead. She grasped the sides of the oak wood podium with vigor as she awaited the judge's decision and her fate. Suddenly the collar on her gray button down shirt felt like a noose tightening around her neck. Mystro quickly removed her right hand from the death grip on the podium; and released her top button, giving herself some immediate relief. She looked away from the judge briefly, and took in her reason for being in court, Leslie Sheppard.

*'Man, she looks like a fucking angel, I wonder if she still has the picture we took at Kings Dominion on her nightstand in the bedroom. I love her so much.'* Mystro thought while looking to her right and gazing upon Leslie.

Leslie could feel the awkward stare coming from her left side, and refused to look in that direction. Mystro's awkwardness was the reason they were in court today. Feeling extremely uncomfortable with Mystro's eyes peering at her, Leslie looked intensely at the judge straight ahead. She wanted this girl out of her life, once and for all, and she prayed he could make that happen.

"Ms. Sheppard, you currently have a Temporary Ex Parte Protection Order, or TPO, in effect against Ms. Malone," Judge Tredall stated. "And you are petitioning the court to have a Civil Protection Order, or CPO, placed in effect for one year, is that correct?"

"Yes, your honor," Leslie replied.

Mystro tuned out the conversation between Judge Tredall and Leslie. She concentrated only on the way Leslie's lips looked while she talked.

"Ms. Sheppard, since you filed for the TPO and it was served, has Ms. Malone continued to harass you in any way that you deem inappropriate?"

"Well, she called me once the police served her the order asking me why I went that far," Leslie testified. "And my co-worker said she thought she saw her car out in front of my job, but I didn't see her. And she had not contacted me after that, your honor."

"Ms. Malone," The judge said trying to get Mystro's attention. "Ms. Malone," the judge yelled again this time banging his gavel.

"Oh, yes, sir." Mystro finally responded breaking out of her stare coma, and facing the judge.

"Young lady, do you understand the severity of this case?"

"I believe so, your honor," Mystro said, stealing another glance at Leslie.

"I don't think you do. We are here today because the petitioner, Ms. Sheppard, has accused you of harassment. She has already been granted a temporary order and I am to determine if a longer protection order is needed," Judge Tredall explained.

"No, sir," Mystro said dropping her head in shame.

"Are you saying an order is not necessary?"

"Yes, sir," Mystro said looking back up at the judge. "I will not contact Leslie anymore. I get it." She looked back at Leslie. This time with tears filling her eyes, as she realized this may be the last time she saw the love of her life. She couldn't believe Leslie took it this far, by throwing their love onto the mercy of the court. Sure Mystro blew up her cell phone and kept showing up at places she knew Leslie would be once they broke up, but she would never harm her. Mystro just wanted to make up, so they could get back together. She was in love.

Mystro studied the details of Leslie's face, she watched the way she kept curling the corners of her pink lips. She knew Leslie did that when she was nervous. She studied the movements of her hands as she talked, and imagined how they used to feel on her back when they made love. She could smell the *Lady Gaga* perfume Leslie wore from where she stood, and thought back to the day she bought it for her at the department store. Mystro thought those were the best times and now, they were all memories.

Leslie continued to look straight ahead as the judge talked to Mystro. She was still unwilling to give her any eye play.

"Ms. Malone, you seem to be a decent young woman with a clean criminal record. Coupled with the fact that you obeyed the Temporary Order, and outside of initial contact, you did not harass Ms. Sheppard."

Mystro blinked back the tears that gathered in her eyes, and turned away from Leslie to give the judge her full attention.

"Therefore, I will vacate the TPO and not grant the CPO," Judge Tredall ruled.

Leslie's shoulders dropped in defeat.

Mystro released a sigh of relief.

"However, it is important that you realize you cannot continue to harass people, Ms. Malone, because this order goes on record. Sometimes we fall in love with people who won't love us back. And it's your job to know the difference, and respect their decision. I never want to see you back here for this type of behavior again. Because you could face serious jail time, do you understand that?"

"Yes, sir, your honor." Mystro replied.

"I hope so, court is now adjourned. Have a good day," Judge Tredall stated slamming his gavel on the block.

Mystro did not move, she stayed put behind the respondent's podium and watched as her ex gathered her belongings and turned to exit the courtroom. As Leslie walked past, Mystro got another whiff of her perfume and her stomach fluttered. All she wanted to do was grab Leslie by the neck, and kiss her back into her life.

"Fuck it," Mystro said, as she trotted out of the courtroom, chasing Leslie.

"Leslie," Mystro yelled attempting to catch her before she left the building.

Leslie stopped, and turned around to face Mystro for the first time all day.

Mystro continued to walk in Leslie's direction while concentrating on her face. She was so excited that Leslie was no longer walking and appeared to be waiting in anticipation of Mystro being in her space again.

*'Maybe she still loves me too. She finally realizes how much she cares, and wants me back.'* Mystro thought, as a small smile crept on her face the closer she got to Leslie. Until she noticed how Leslie's face went from anticipation to anger.

"Mystro Mason, I…do…not…want…you anymore. Stay far away from me or I will put your stalking, psychotic ass in jail," Leslie yelled out into the court building's hallway. Several on-lookers took notice, before turning and walking out the door.

Mystro stopped dead in her tracks in defeat. She felt like she was going to be sick. Maybe their love affair was really over after all.

# CHAPTER 1

"Damn, girl you got me throbbing like shit," Native said. "It's the perfect time and we in the perfect place. Just let me feel how wet it is," Native continued kissing her prospect on the neck.

"Mmmm," Supervisor Jones moaned. "You right, it is the perfect time, because I'm horny too, but it's not the right place. We at work and I'm your manager," she explained to Native inside the dressing room of the shoe store.

It was an extremely slow Saturday afternoon in the popular tennis shoe haven. Normally Saturdays meant action in, and action out of the store, but not today. The emptiness gave Native the brilliant idea to try her hand at seducing her boss, who often flirted with her on the regular.

"Come on, Supe, we good right now. Mystro got the floor on lock. Nobody coming back here. I got all the time in the world to make you weak," Native continued to plead.

"You not going to just fuck me and cross my name off your list like the rest of them bitches. I'm not having it!"

"Boo, I been digging on you for a long time. You sexy as shit, you smart, beautiful and most importantly you my boss. That authority you hold is the main reason I gotta have you," Native stated, as she squeezed Supervisor Jones' left breast. "And I promise that you won't be unsatisfied. So what you trying to do?"

"Give me a second to think," Supervisor Jones said pushing her back.

Native stopped, and begin to smooth out her green uniform shirt. She really wanted and intended to fuck her manager right there. But, she knew continuing to beg was not in her profile. If Native was going to get in that ass, it would be because Jones wanted her just as badly.

"I'm waiting," Native said.

Supervisor Jones looked at her watch, and saw it was three-o'clock in the afternoon. She knew that her night shift crew would not be in until five-o'clock. She also knew it was slow out in the store, and that Native's best friend Mystro, who worked with them, was able to handle any customers who decided to shop.

Truth be told, outside of the comforts of Supervisor Jones' own home, this was as good as it was going to get. So, Jones made up her mind to give in to temptation.

Jones studied Native and took her in. She loved Native's Indian straight jet-black hair, which she kept in two French braids that hung over her shoulders. She could not take her eyes off of Native's mocha complexion, that played host to all twelve of the tattoo's strategically placed all over her body. But the deal closer was Native's white bright smile that melted her loins every time Jones saw it. Oh yeah, she was ready to fuck!

Native watched as Jones began to unbutton her polo shirt that displayed the company's logo. She immediately began to snatch her own shirt off, excited that she was about to get the cheeks. As Jones removed her shirt, Native noticed that her white bra strap looked a little dingy. It wasn't bad enough to make Native stop her pursuit, but she did make mental notes of it. To avoid seeing any more dirty underclothes, she quickly pulled Jones toward her.

"Native, did you make sure the door was locked?" Jones whispered looking up from their embrace.

"Yeah, ma, I ain't slow. No more talking," Native said before she pushed Jones into the wall passionately, and pressed her body against hers. "It's time to get down to business."

The two tongued each other down, while Native explored all over Jones's curves. Against her better judgment, and in the heat of the moment, Native snatched up Jones' dirty bra and began to suck her nipples. She loved how they immediately became hard inside her mouth. She spent time flicking her tongue back and fourth between Jones' left and right nipple.

Jones was so turned on that she felt warm cream escape her pussy that was still housed inside her thong and pants. She needed relief and she wanted it now. After all, she had secretly wanted Native since the first day she saw her face.

No longer able to control herself, Native began to unbuckle Jones' belt, and yank at her khaki Dockers. While still kissing her deeply, Native slid her index and middle finger around Jones' thong and into her hairy pussy. Although the bush was a little more than Native preferred, or expected, Jones was extremely wet. This alone sent Native into overdrive, and she dismissed the imperfection.

"Sit down, Supe."

She took a seat on the wooden bench.

"I'm 'bout to send you to the—," Native stopped dead in her tracks. Something was off. *Way off.*

"Mmmmm, I can't wait," Jones said not feeling Native's distance. "Please don't keep me in suspense. I wanna feel your tongue inside me," Jones anxiously begged. "I want you to lick my pussy up." She was oblivious to Native's mood change.

"You know what, this ain't right," Native said, while backing up and straightening her uniform once again.

"What are you talking about? What ain't right?" Jones asked confused with her legs open, and bare ass on the dressing room's wooden bench.

"How the fuck can you be a grown woman in your thirties, and walk around with your pussy smelling like garbage truck juice?" Native boldly questioned. She was furious that her face almost went there.

"O-M-GEEE! Are you fucking kidding me," Jones shot back, highly upset and embarrassed.

"You don't smell that shit?" Native questioned.

"What do you mean," she sniffed the air. "It smells like sex to me."

"Supe, I don't know what kinda sex you use to, but it ain't never 'sposed to smell like this shit," Native schooled.

"I have never in my life been told no bullshit like this! And trust me, I have had plenty sex partners."

"Yeah, that's exactly what it smell like too! Your pussy is rancid! You may have the clap or some shit. You need to seek medical attention to clear that up pronto," Native continued, heading towards the door to leave.

"You got me fucked up, dyke! I knew I shouldn't have gotten involved with your ass," Jones yelled pulling up her thong and pants.

Native walked out of the dressing room, leaving Jones to her anger and pussy odor. When she hit the sales floor she locked eyes with her best friend Mystro.

Mystro was busy closing a sales purchase with a customer when she approached. "Son, smell this shit," Native demanded, not caring that the customer had not left the counter, when she shoved her fingers under Mystro's nose.

"Uggh, nigga. Go 'head wit' that shit. The fuck is that?" Mystro questioned wiping her upper lip.

"It's Supe. That bitch snatch rotten."

Mystro fell out in laughter, which made Native angrier. "That shit ain't funny, man. What the fuck? I hate for bitches not to be hygienic. She had a dingy bra on and everything. That was my fault for not dipping when I peeped that," Native confessed.

The customer who should have been gone by now, was taking her time leaving out the store. Her ear hustle antennas had been activated, and she tried her hardest to listen to as much as possible as she slowly made an exit.

"Wooooowww…That's terrible. She too sexy for that shit," Mystro added. "But come on, champ you need to be easy. I need my job. You know I'm saving up for my own spot. I got a five year plan."

"Ohhh my god, if I gotta hear about that damn five year plan again, I'ma shoot somebody." Native said frustrated.

"I'm serious, moe, relax for you get us fired."

"Yeah aight, you right. I mean even though I got sponsors to get me fresh, if I don't kick mommy her money, I'm gonna be homeless."

"Right 'cuz you ain't moving in the spot with me and my future wife, whenever I get one." Mystro said.

Native rolled her eyes.

Just then Supervisor Jones came out onto the sales floor. She watched as the customer was leaving, but continued to look back towards Native and Mystro's direction. She saw how Native stood behind the counter with Mystro, while they both were laughing, probably at her. The scene infuriated her even more.

She walked up to them. "You fired. Both of you. Get out now," Jones yelled.

"Fired?" Both Native and Mystro replied.

"Yes, I didn't stutter. I want you gone, immediately. Don't bother clocking out."

"How the fuck you gonna fire us?" Native asked.

"Right, I ain't even did shit, Supe," Mystro followed up.

"I can fire whoever the fuck I want. I run this shop. Ya'll two dykes been stealing from this company for too long. I just been letting ya'll get away with it, but that's dead," Jones fabricated.

"Mannnn, prove it," Native challenged.

While Native wanted Jones to produce evidence, Mystro knew they had been side-selling unreleased Jordan's and Nike Foamposites at higher prices, for extra profit for a minute. The problem was that everyone did it, including Supervisor Jones. They had a specific list of people they sold to, and they would all make a come up on the fact that these people would damn near pay anything just to have the exclusive shoes early. But given the circumstances that had just taken place, Mystro knew Native and her were finished there.

Mystro immediately took off her nametag and walked into the back to retrieve their things.

"Do you really want me to show you my evidence, Native? Or better yet, how about I just show the police?" Jones threatened.

Native thought about Supe's words. She also knew they participated in fraudulent activity. And she figured what Mystro figured, it was better to just get fired, than it was to get fired and arrested. So Native didn't say another word. She just snatched her polo off revealing her white wife beater, and numerous tattoos. Just as she threw her shirt on the floor, Mystro came around the corner with her book bag and tossed Native her's.

"Let's break out," Mystro instructed.

Native put her Nike book bag on her back, and adjusted the navy Washington Nationals baseball cap on her head. She followed Mystro towards the door just as a group of dudes were walking inside the store. Native saw the opportunity as payback time. Standing at the store's entrance, she looked at the guys, and then at Jones.

"Next time you wanna get fucked in the dressing room, make sure you wash your ass," Native yelled. "No woman should smell like she got a trout between her legs, ever. Fuck you, bitch." Native laughed, as she and Mystro strolled out of the mall in hysterics.

Supervisor Jones stood there motionless and mortified as the group of young baller's laughed uncontrollably at Native's comment. Jones ignored the guys, and continued to stare at Native's back, as she disappeared out of the mall.

*That dyke has to come back and pick up her last check. And as soon as she does, I'ma have something for her ass.* Supervisor Jones thought.

# CHAPTER 2

"Getting fired really fucking wit' my pockets, son," Native told Mystro. "I need some income fast. Mommy already on my back for the rent."

"Humph…your ass wasn't too concerned when we was at work. You know you ain't have no business trying to get at Supe. You don't be thinking, nigga," Mystro shot back. "You set me back wit' that dumb shit."

It had been three weeks after they were fired. Being as though they left on bad terms, Mystro came up with the idea that included her going to their former job on Supervisor Jones' off day, to retrieve her and Native's last check. She figured Jones would never turn over their money without a problem. With the new plan in play, Mystro was able to walk into the store, and pick up their checks from the assistant manager, minus any dramatic scene that Supe would've given.

Mystro and Native were at Native's mother's house, where they shared a medium sized bedroom in the Northeast section of Washington DC. Although Native was still unemployed, Mystro was able to get a job at *Hoagies Sandwich Shop*. She was serious about building a future and a family, complete with a beautiful wife and she knew having an income was key.

"Slim, there was no way I knew all that was happening in her draws. You even admitted she was a bad bitch that was well put together. I mean she stayed coming to work smelling like expensive perfume. I'da been a fool to not try and smash. 'Specially after all the love she was throwing a nigga."

"Well congratulations, champ. You got the green light but now what?" Mystro questioned facetiously.

"Man, fuck her and that job. I hate working for another mothafucka anyway. We need to start snatching shit like I been telling you we should do," Native answered.

Ever since they became friends in high school, which was over ten years ago, Native was always trying to get Mystro to be a part of some caper. From boosting clothes and movies, to pre-selling high priced shoes and robbing people, Native thought about it all. Some of the schemes they even followed through with. The only problem was neither one of them really had the heart for crime. Although Native made up for what heart she lacked, with her extreme determination. Mystro, on the other hand, was not a fan of the criminal lifestyle.

"Man, you know I ain't 'bout to fuck with you on no stick ups. I feel bad enough about the shoe shit. I like to get my ends honestly, you know that," Mystro confessed, while getting dressed.

"Shut your bamma ass up! You always acting like you ain't got no hustle in you. I know that's bullshit though cuz you was cut from the same cloth as me, so kill all that noise," Native hollered.

"Whatever, I gotta get ready to break out, son," Mystro informed.

"The fuck you going so early?"

"Gotta get to work. I can't keep sitting around wit' you trying to cook up schemes."

"Whatever, nigga. I know you ain't trying to retire in no hoagie shop."

"Fuck no," Mystro laughed, "but for now, it's paying the bills. You know your mother gonna keep coming at us sideways until she got her money. Plus you know I got a plan to stick to. They still hiring. You need to come through that joint and get an app," Mystro informed.

"Naw, I'ma leave the bread baking and foot long making to your ass," Native teased.

"Hahaha...Suck my dick," Mystro joked, "What you gonna do about PRIDE. though? I know you need a new fit or two for the parties."

"Oh, my nigga, you know I ain't gonna have no problem scaring some sponsors up to at least hook me up a few pieces to wear. You dig?" Native said arrogantly.

"I feel you," Mystro laughed, "But what you gonna have to do to get that sponsorship is the question? You remember the last time you had to pass out a charity fuck right," Mystro chastised. "You still got that restraining order in effect on ole girl?"

"Everybody a mothafucking comedian these days I guess," Native said angrily. "At least I was the one that had to put the order out on a bitch and not the one the order was put on." Native shot back referring to the TPO Leslie placed on Mystro some months back.

Mystro did not reply, she just looked away from Native with sadness in her eyes thinking about Leslie.

"My bad, son, I went too far. I ain't mean to-" Native's apology was interrupted by a loud bang at the front door. The two friends dashed down the charcoal gray-carpeted stairs, and looked through the window. On the other side of it stood their protégé' who they affectionately named, Baby Dom. All five-foot-nothing inches of herself.

Mystro opened the door. "Baby Dom, what the fuck you banging for, Champ," Mystro questioned.

"Right, you know mommy upstairs trying to sleep before church tonight," Native scolded.

"Oh…damn…my bad…Fam," Baby Dom said, clearly out of breath.

"I…was…trying…to…see…what ya'll…was up…to…and shit," she continued, as she dropped her head down, and grabbed her basketball shorts at the knees while looking anxiously to her left.

"What we was up to? Get the hell outta here," Mystro yelled unenthused.

"Yeah, and why you keep looking back and fourth? What the fuck is up?" Native asked her.

"Nothing...nothing, just...out jogging and shit, ain't no whole lot to that," Baby Dom replied, looking up at the two and trying to regain her breath.

"Jogging? Not wit' them foam's on your feet, your ass begged and schemed for us to get you. I know better than that. You wouldn't even ball in 'em, much less be fake jogging. Stop bullshitting," Mystro schooled.

"For real, I wouldn't lie to ya'll. You like family to me." Baby Dom tried to convince them of her honesty, while she continuously peered over her shoulder, and down the street.

"You welling, I can tell," Native added.

"Uh...I gotta use the bathroom. Let me come in right quick, Fam," Baby Dom said now standing, as she begin to shift her weight from her left to her right foot, in an attempt to look as though she really had to pee.

"Hell no," both Mystro and Native yelled simultaneously.

"You know you can't get past the porch 'round here, wit' your thieving ass," Mystro advised.

"Oh naw, come on, Fam. I ain't 'bout that life no more," Baby Dom said bending back down and panting while looking off the porch and into the street again.

"Fuck you mean you ain't 'bout that life? The last time we let you come through, Native was a pair of J's lighter. You forget 'bout that?" Mystro asked.

"Oh naw…Shit, I was young and tripping. Know what I'm saying," She replied, "that wasn't personal. I was just practicing."

"*Young*?" Mystro leaned in. "BD, that was six months ago."

"Right, and she tried to sell me back my own shit the next day," Native stated. "After we spanked dat ass, we told you no more invites into the crib."

In the not so far distance gunshots, and a man yelling could be heard up the street. He was the local street vender who sold everything at his table from fake NFL jersey's, to fake Timberland boots. It was your choice, but they would always be fake.

"Where the fuck is that lil dyke bitch," Stand Dude yelled, angrily while occasionally introducing his .9mm's bullets into the air.

Now standing up straight again Baby Dom faced them and said, "Fam, unless you want us all to be killed, I think ya'll need to let me in."

# CHAPTER 3

Mystro walked into the Hoagie shop where she currently worked. She hated the way the store always smelled. Although, it was the scent of fresh bread baking, it became nauseating to her, but it was a job so she had to deal with it.

"Chocolate, Mr. Kadam here with the checks yet?" Mystro asked her co-worker who stood behind the counter doing nothing.

"Yeah, he here, in the back. Hey, how you get off for a weekend already? You only been working here for a couple weeks." Chocolate sounded disgruntled.

"I put in for it when I got hired. Why you in my business?"

Mystro couldn't stand Chocolate. When she first got the job, she tried to be cool with her. But, she soon discovered that Chocolate wanted what Mystro did not want with her, a relationship. Although Mystro really wanted to be wifed up with a family, she still had taste. Chocolate was annoying. She would do simple shit like brush past Mystro as she made customer's sandwiches and pinch her butt. And the worst was when she showed off in front of pretty customers that Mystro was trying to rap to.

She did it purposely to cock block, and shut her business down.

Mystro had no other option she had to be direct with her. She didn't understand anything else, but she still tried.

"I'm asking, because I got tickets for the Kanye West concert next Saturday," Chocolate continued. "You trying to go with me?"

"Fuck no," Mystro answered. "Ain't trynna step out with you, you know that."

"You need to be a little more friendly," Chocolate advised. "You might need me sooner than you think."

"I'm good," Mystro said, walking past the cream counter. She headed toward the back office.

"Hmph…we'll see," Chocolate added.

Before Mystro reached the back office, she could tell her boss was in there. The strong scent of Indian cuisine tickled her nose hairs. The aroma threatened to have Mystro recycle her breakfast. She pushed through anyway, and gently knocked on the closed steel office door.

"Come in," Mr. Kadam stated.

Mystro walked inside. "How you doing, sir? I came to get my check, is it ready?" Mystro politely asked.

"Yes, yes, Mystro. I have it for you. Come in, and sit. I must speak with you."

*Damn, I ain't sign up for all this shit.* Mystro thought. "Yes, sir," she said as she sat in the empty chair across from Mr. Kadam's desk.

"I know you requested this weekend off, but I need you to work. Chocolate has a previous engagement, and since she has seniority, I have given her off," Mr. Kadam informed, in his heavy accent, as he shuffled through the white envelopes nervously, never looking up.

When he found Mystro's paycheck, he handed it to her with his right hand, while pushing his black-rimmed bifocals up on his face with his left hand. Finally he gazed upon Mystro's face awaiting her reaction to the bad news.

"Mr. Kadam, with all due respect, I have a prior commitment as well. I mentioned it in my interview, before I even took the job. You telling me it was cool was the only reason I was able to accept this position, over another offer I had."

"I wish there was more I could do for you, but hands are tied."

"Sir, this is throwing my plans off."

"But Chocolate asked for time yesterday."

"And, I asked for the time three weeks ago."

"I understand your concern, but I need one of you here, and since she has been here longer, it is her who can be off. I hope you understand," he replied.

Mystro took her silver and blue Dallas Cowboys cap off her head, exposing her fuzzy cornrows, and wiped her forehead trying to calm herself down. After a brief pause, she placed her cap back on and said, "Maybe I can work a couple of hours. And, Chocolate can cover for me later."

"No she needs whole day."

Mystro frowned. "You telling me this the day before my event. You not even willing to work with me?"

"She needs whole day, end of discussion," he yelled. "Be here tomorrow!"

Mystro was stuck, but what else could she do?

"It's cool, Mr. K. I'll be here, no worries," Mystro responded convincingly. She got up and glided towards the door. "I'll see you tomorrow."

"Great, 7:00am," Mr. Kadam finished. "Mystro, perhaps if you ask Chocolate nicely, she'll work for you."

Mystro was in a bind. She wanted desperately to move into her own apartment. She was grateful to Native and her mother for looking out for her, when her father got sick and she had nowhere to go; but it was time to grow up and get her own place. Quitting her job, at this point, would set her back in accomplishing that goal. She really had to consider her decision before making any moves, especially in haste. Although Mystro was beyond burnt up, she refused to let her anger take center stage, when she walked past Chocolate.

As she rounded the corner, debating in her mind whether or not to ask her to work, she locked eyes with her. Her overbearing ass-coworker matched her stare, as she outlined her lips from top to bottom with her index finger and thumb of her right hand.

"You sure you don't wanna be my date to the concert? My plans this weekend can change, if you give me a reason." She ran her tongue over her lips.

*Fuck this shit.* She thought.

In that moment, Mystro knew two things. One was that Chocolate sucked Mr. Kadam off for a work free weekend, and two, both them motherfuckas would be there playing with each others parts, when Mystro didn't show up tomorrow.

The only thing was now, she was gonna have to find yet another job.

* * * **TWO HOURS LATER** * * *

"Sit still, My," Breezy said, "your hair gonna be crooked if you keep squirming."

"Man, you know my ass falling asleep. I will never understand why I gotta always sit on this hard ass wooden floor under you, just to get tightened up. Why can't you use the stylist chair? That's what its sposed to be for," Mystro inquired as she adjusted her position.

Mystro cashed her check, and was now at her friend Breezy's apartment getting her hair braided. It was the weekend of gay pride in Washington D.C., which meant hanging out in the city day and night. Mystro had to be fresh, starting with her hair. Mystro was a neat freak, who took pride in her appearance. This meant she had to get her hair braided every two weeks, but for this weekend's special events, she had to be extra sharp.

"You know I can grip it better when you sit on the floor," Breezy explained. "Besides, I know you like sliding between these thighs, so stop faking."

"I do huh?" Mystro flirted.

"Mmm hmm…So I just gotta give you what you want. And why you getting all extra dapper anyway? I just did your rows five days ago. They wasn't even that fuzzy."

"I don't know if you know or not, but PRIDE this weekend. I can't be nowhere in these streets looking the fuck terrible," Mystro explained.

"PRIDE? I never pegged you as a parade marcher. Why are you burdening yourself with all them queens and dykes?" Breezy asked, with a jealous undertone.

"Slim, ain't nobody 'bout to be marching in no damn parade. Truthfully, I'd rather be kicking it in a hotel with my shawty, than going out to fuck with the faggies and shit. But Native wanna hang and you know we a team, so we roll twolo," Mystro advised.

"That's a mess. You need to tell her you ain't trying to go. Although, you might as well cuz it ain't like you got no shawty to kick it with no more, right?" Breezy asked nosily.

Mystro paused before she answered her question and sighed. "Naw, not no more," she sad sadly.

"Oh, well that's good. Bitches is scandalous in these streets. You already ahead by being by yourself as far as I'm concerned," Breezy said noticing her friends mode change.

Mystro sat in silence. Thoughts of Leslie danced through her mind and brought with them pain and hurt. She would give anything to talk to her again, to find out where she went wrong.

She tilted her head to the left, to allow Breezy to finish her last braid.

When she was done, Breezy exhaled. "That's it, babes. Run me my ends, suga," Breezy demanded jokingly.

"Oh you know I don't even move like that. I got you," Mystro said breaking out of her thoughts. She peeled off a twenty-dollar bill from her stack, followed by a ten-dollar bill for Breezy's tip. She handed both bills to her.

Mystro stretched her five foot nine inch frame completely, by standing up with outstretched arms into the air. She was relieved her ass no longer had to date the hardwood floor. She slowly walked over to the mirror that rested on the dresser to peep her braids. Mystro's honey brown complexion peered back at her, as she studied her hair. She brushed the back of her grey Levis jeans off, before giving verbal approval of Breezy's work.

"You did me right, thanks, B. Now, I gotta go get up with my nigga to go shopping. You need anything before I dip though?" Mystro asked.

"No, boy...I mean girl, I'm good. You so sweet for asking though," Breezy informed, staring up into Mystro's hazel eyes.

This was not the first time Mystro had been called a boy. Although she is a woman, and never had any desires on being a man, because she dressed in a masculine fashion, people made the mistake frequently. But it didn't bother her. She thought it was funny.

"Aight, so I'll see you soon. Thanks again," Mystro said as she bent down and gripped Breezy in a tight embrace, lifting her five-five frame off the floor. Mystro slid Breezy a kiss on her cheek, and placed her back down before walking out of the apartment door.

As Mystro pressed down the hallway of the apartment building, her mind drifted back to Breezy. She thought Breezy was smart, sexy and had a brain. She said Breezy had what she called, The Full Court Press. Which meant full luscious lips, full round titties, full fat ass, and a full set of white teeth. She thought she could be wifey material, and would love nothing more than to date her. But there were two problems. One, Mystro could become very obsessed when it came to the women she dated. She had huge plans of finding a woman to marry and have kids with to complete her family. And she would do anything in her power to make that happen. But, ever since she had papers put out on her for being a stalker, she had to try and control her impulsive behavior when it came to women.

Two, Breezy wasn't even gay. She was on niggas, although most of them never stayed around long. She always seemed to find something wrong with them, before letting them go.

Mystro made it outside to her older model black Nissan Maxima, and hit the un-lock button on her viper remote. She accidently dropped her keys. She bent down to retrieve them, when out of the corner of her right eye, she saw a set of grey New Balance tennis shoes quickly approaching her. By the time she stood up to get in her car, Mr. New Balance was on her back, with his glock poking her spine.

"Look, this can be quick and easy, or quick and final for you. I don't want your life or your ride, but I will take your paper," he whispered into Mystro's ear. He was so close she felt his dick on her butt. She felt violated in more ways than one. "How you want it, young?"

"Man...Fuck. Aight, cuz, don't do no bamma shit," Mystro said calmly as she slowly raised her hands in the air to show she was not a threat. "It's in my front right pocket, " She informed. "I'ma get it for you."

"Hurry up, shawty. I ain't trying to slump you out here but I will," he continued.

Mystro was a ball of emotions. She was nervous and fearful, but at the same time she was calm and angry. She wasn't just mad she was being robbed, she was mad at herself for parking in the bad neighborhood in an alley.

With no other choice, she reached into her pocket and retrieved her remaining cash. She raised the wad of cash up, and leaned it back into the jacker's direction reluctantly.

He snatched the money and said, "Thanks, Shawty Be Bop. Don't look so sad, you get to live," he laughed as he ran out of Mystro's life just as fast as he entered it.

Mystro stood there defeated, depressed and $685 lighter. But she looked good though.

* * * 30 **MINUTES LATER** * * *

Mystro pulled onto her street and began to parallel park her car. Once parked, she approached the steps leading to her house where she saw Native and Baby Dom on the porch talking.

Not noticing the glum look on Mystro's face, Native pulled her into their conversation. "Son, this lil nigga still trying to cop a plea 'bout snatching them bogus ass Timbo's off slim's stand last month. She don't understand that she can't go around taking shit from people she know, playing or not. We almost got shot fucking with her. Had you not given that nigga a bill to shut his ass up, he woulda blasted on us. 'Specially you, Baby Dom," Native schooled.

"I know, I know, Fam. It won't happen again, either. That shit jive spooked me," Baby Dom admitted.

"We'll see," Native replied, "You ready to hit the mall, Mystro?"

"Slim, I got jacked leaving Breezy spot. The nigga got me for my whole paycheck. I can't go get shit with no money," Mystro explained sadly.

"Oh fuck no, Fam. Let's tool up and ride back through there," Baby Dom said extra hype.

"Tool up? Get your baby nut ass off this porch with that shit," Mystro shot back, "Ain't nobody riding through no gang neighborhood to get back no money. I ain't even see the nigga's face that got me anyway."

"Yeah, beat it, Baby Dom, I gotta rap to my nigga." Native directed.

Baby Dom jumped up, and sadly walked off the porch and up the street.

As if things couldn't get any worse, Margaret, Native's mother, opened the screen door and yelled, "Do ya'll got my damn rent money?" The pink muumuu she wore stank of mothballs and White Diamonds perfume.

"Mommy, come on man," Native said looking around the sunny neighborhood, "go back in the house with that shit on. It's daylight, people can still see you out here."

"I don't give a fuck, I want my money got damn it," she yelled. "Now where the fuck is it?" She eyeballed both of them, waiting for an answer.

Although the rent was only one hundred dollars a-piece, she may as well have been asking for fifteen hundred, since they were currently both broke and unemployed.

"We'll have your money for you tonight," Native promised.

"I'm coming to your room later for my cash, and don't be a penny short," she walked back into the house and the screen door slammed behind her.

"Fuck," Native yelled.

"If slim hadn't relieved me of my paper, we would've been good," Mystro said.

"Check this out, son, I know we may not be go hard enough to go back and get what was taken from you, but we damn sure can make our own come up on somebody else," Native suggested.

Mystro took a moment to think before she answered. Normally, she was not with the hair-brained-quick-money schemes that Native proposed. But today, she felt beaten and she was broke. To top it all off, Margaret wanted her rent money and she was taking no excuses. Plus, Mystro knew she wasn't going back to the Hoagie shop ever again. So, after much deliberation, she looked at her friend and asked, "What's your plan?"

# CHAPTER 4

"I ain't too sure 'bout this, Nae." Mystro confessed.

"You not sure 'bout what, son?" Native asked, annoyed.

"This shit...we actually 'bout to do the same thing to someone that was done to me a few hours ago. Shit ain't cool," Mystro stated.

"Slim, what else you wanna do," Native turned around to face Mystro from the passenger seat. "We trying to party tonight, but now we empty and we gotta pay rent on top of it all. Plus, this the weekend we been waiting on all year," Native pleaded.

"Naw, champ, this the weekend you been waiting on. I just go cuz I know you be hype 'bout it. You know I hate the club scene," Mystro explained.

"What the fuck? So now you tell me? Look, son, you ain't gotta do nothing you don't want to for real," Native spat. "I'ma big girl, I can roll solo," she continued.

"Fuck is you getting all in your feelings for?" Mystro asked turning her head to her left to address Native.

"I'm not in my feelings, son, I'm just saying. You ain't never said nothing 'bout not wanting to hit the club for PRIDE before. Now just cuz we gotta put in a little work for some money, you hesitating." She looked back out onto the parking lot.

Mystro knew her nerves were getting the best of her. She needed to calm down and come clean with her friend instead of making excuses. "Look, we ain't gotta come undone. My bad, I just feel off. I ain't never held up nobody before," Mystro said.

"I know, man, I know...me neither," Native turned to look at her friend. "But we ain't gonna hurt nobody. We ain't even got no bullets, remember?"

Mystro nodded, and continued to check her surroundings from the driver's seat of her Maxima. She reflected back to an hour ago when she and Native rummaged through the attic in an attempt to locate Native's uncle's gun. After thirty minutes of searching, they finally recovered the .32 caliber firearm. However, it was not loaded, and after another fifteen minutes, they could not locate one bullet.

"So we just gonna lay here and look for the most unaware person, who look like they got some gwaup, and we roll up. Simple," Native coached.

"Fuck man. This shit can't be right," Mystro continued to whine.

"Nigga, stop bitching up," Native barked, having tired of Mystro's sulking. "If you do it and it don't sit well with you, I won't ask you no more. But, I need you today, right now. Got me?" Native bargained.

Mystro looked straight ahead through the windshield. She watched different people coming in and out of the PG Plaza food court entrance of the mall. The blasting air condition, and the nervous thoughts of armed robbery, made tiny goose bumps appear all over her bare arms. She glanced to her right at Native briefly and could see anticipation in her eyes. Mystro knew that if she did this and something went wrong, they could get hurt or caught. But, she also knew if she didn't do it, Native would move without her and not have anyone watching her back. Mystro's downfall at times was her loyalty. She knew this could possibly not end well, but she gave her word and that was something she did not take lightly.

There was no more debating; she knew what had to be done. "Native, we—,"

Before Mystro could finish her statement, Native jumped out of the car and slammed the door. Mystro looked on in shock and anger, as she studied Native run up on a female walking in the parking lot. '*I know this mothafucka not 'bout to bank shawty without me.*' Mystro thought. It wasn't until she remembered the gun was still under the passenger seat, that she calmed down a little. '*What the fuck is she doing?*' Mystro pondered as she watched closely.

* * * **PARKING LOT** * * *

"Excuse me, ma…you dropped something," Native yelled jogging up on the woman.

The bronzed Brazilian looking female turned around to look behind her, but didn't see anything on the ground.

"What did I drop?" she asked.

"My number," Native said, sounding corny as shit. '*If she smiles she mine.*' Native thought.

She smiled.

"I never had your number to drop, honey," Brazilian Chick said, blushing.

"Girl, stop playing. Let me check your phone," Native played harder.

"Give you my phone? No boo, you not about to trot off with my Blackberry and have me standing out here looking ridiculous."

"Naw, ma. I ain't that nigga. Here," Native dug into the pocket of her fatigue cargo shorts, and pulled out her iPhone. "You hold my phone while I put my number in yours," Native said, holding her phone in her hand.

"You real bold, how you even know I want your number?" Brazilian Chick asked.

"Cuz I know you wanna keep a smile on your beautiful face, and I can do that for you," Native bragged, and winked her right eye.

"You think you so smooth, don't you?"

"Naw, I'm just being straight with you. I think you gorgeous and would love to take you out and show you a good time." Native put it all on the line.

Brazilian Chick laughed. "So, is this your thing, hanging out in mall parking lots to look for women?"

Native smiled. "Naw, ma, me and my homie just pulled up and was looking for a parking space when I spotted you." She lied. "What about you, for some reason you don't look like you'd shop in this type of mall?"

"No, I don't really. But I had to get some special hair color for a client of mine this afternoon and only the beauty store here carried it." She explained.

"Oh, ok, so you a stylist?"

"Yes."

"That's what's up," Native said nervously. "So, what you say, shawty, you gonna give me your number?"

Brazilian Chick did not say anything.

Native watched her closely and observed how she looked her up and down. Then proceeded to check out the rest of the parking lot to see who was looking. When she was finished, she reached into her brown Michael Kors bag, and pulled out her blackberry. She handed the phone to Native.

Native immediately punched in her code to unlock her iPhone and handed it to her. "You know how to program your number in my phone?" Native inquired.

"Yes, I used to have an iPhone," she informed. "But I upgraded," she joked.

Native watched as the Brazilian Chick punched numbers into her contact. She took a long look at her. Shawty was banging, she had the prettiest feet Native ever saw. She immediately started to visualize how it would be to fuck her.

"Well, when you done, can you assist me with your phone?" Native asked. "I ain't had a blackberry in about five years, so I feel jive remedial over here," she confessed.

Brazilian Chick laughed and handed Native her iPhone back. She then leaned in so close to Native that her shoulder rested against Native's bare shoulder. She proceeded to guide Native through her blackberry.

"You smell good as shit. What kinda perfume you got on?" Native inquired.

"Thank you," she smiled. "It's called, *Miami Glow* by J. Lo."

"Damn, that's my new favorite perfume now," Native added for free. "Well, I don't wanna keep you from your appointment any longer. But it was a pleasure to meet you—"

"Brisa," Brazilian Chick said, extending her hand to shake Native's.

Native reached out and grabbed Brisa's hand and said, "Brisa, that's pretty. And it's a very fitting name. I'm Native."

"Very nice meeting you too, Native."

"I'll give you a call...And, Brisa, when we hook up, make sure you wear that perfume," Native said releasing her hand, giving her one more wink for the road.

Brisa smiled and turned to walk to her car.

\* \* \* **BACK IN THE MAXIMA**\* \* \*

"Are you serious, young?" Mystro asked, as Native jumped back into the passenger seat and slammed the door. "Are you playing with me or what?"

"What?" Native said.

"Did you just jump the fuck out and book a broad in the middle of our caper?"

"Hell yeah. Did you see her? You got me fucked all the way up if you thought I was letting that pass by, slim. *Shitttt*, I love bad bitches that's my fuckin' problem!" Native sang.

"Moe, you go smack at anything," Mystro chastised letting Native know that she peeps how Native will rap to any girl. "Let's get this shit done before you book another chick that can identify your ass in a lineup," Mystro said angrily.

"Aight, man, pull around the back of the mall," Native informed. "Not that many people park back there."

Mystro put the car in drive and proceeded to steer to the back of the mall. The night sky now covered the windows. It was completely dark outside. When they reached the back, they posted up across the parking lot, away from the mall.

"Aight, kill the engine, son," Native instructed.

Mystro cut the car off and took the key out of the ignition.

"Now, we watch and wait," Native continued.

"Hand me the roc," Mystro said. "I need my drunk muscles."

Native handed her the pint-sized bottle, and Mystro downed a big gulp of peach Ciroc straight. She handed it back to Native for her to do the same. She did.

"My nigga, when we see somebody that can get got, auto start the car and we gonna jump out. Then make sure you lock the door back with the key and not the alarm," Native coached. "So when we trying to get back in, won't no alarm sounds come on bringing unwanted attention, and no hot ass engine starting."

Mystro was in shock. "You sure you ain't never done this before?" She asked. "Cuz you got the intricate details down to a science."

"Fuck ass no, but I watch a lot of shit and you know a nigga is well read," Native explained. "Plus, some shit just common sense."

Mystro reached into the back seat and grabbed the two black zipped hooded sweatshirts. She tossed Native one and proceeded to put the other one over her head carefully so she didn't fuzz up her braids. Native grabbed the .32 from under the passenger seat, and let it rest in her lap.

"Look," Native pointed ahead, "I see a mark. Lace up, let's roll."

Mystro threw her Do Rag on and pulled her hood up over her head before jumping out of the car. She closed and locked the door behind her as instructed, and simultaneously hit the auto start button on her viper.

Native was fast across the parking lot on a mission already. Mystro caught up to her, and repeatedly looked around as they advanced on their target. Native was also checking to make sure there were no potential witnesses.

Directly in their sight was an unsuspecting female. She looked to be in her late thirties, give or take five years. She had two big shopping bags in one hand, and she was busy bumping her gums on her cell phone with the other. She stopped at a late model BMW, and appeared to be searching for her keys, never pausing her conversation once. Until, she looked up and saw two black hoodies and a gun ten feet away from her. She let out a blood-curdling scream.

"I know you not 'bout to rob me," she yelled out in a ghetto twang. "Get the fuck away from me," she continued to scream, while swinging her bags wildly towards her would be attackers.

Like clockwork, a mall security guard doing his rounds in his patrol jeep, bent the corner and observed the scene. He rushed in their direction and to the victim's rescue.

# CHAPTER 5

Native was in the bathroom at home taking a shit, with the door wide open. She had a thing about closing the door while on the toilet. She felt if the door was shut, she might miss out on a whole lot of nothing going on in the rest of the house. As she sat there scrolling through her flickgram page on her iPhone, she paused when she heard her mother call her name from the other room. Maybe this was the action she was waiting on.

"Native Houston," Margret yelled. "Shut that damn bathroom door. I'm tired of smelling your shit while I'm trying to cook. It's nasty and uncouth. Flush the toilet and spray."

"Ma...my shit smells like apples," Native yelled while laughing, and placing her cell phone down on the cold tiled floor before flushing the toilet.

"Like rotten damn apples. Now shut that door."

"Aight...Aight," Native replied giving in to her mother.

As she wrapped up her daily contribution to the plumbing, she heard Mystro step out of the bedroom, and move toward the bathroom. So she opened the door again.

"Native, hurry up off that bowl, young. You funking up the whole upstairs. I need you to snap my picture right quick," Mystro advised.

"Damn, moe, I see you was able to come up with a fit. I thought you was still in that joint tripping off almost getting caught at the mall," Native teased.

"Oh, I'm tripping but you the one that came slam in here and took a shit," Mystro shot back. "I guess your guts let you down," she laughed. "And keep your voice down too, for your mother hear you. She liable to grill you out then make you go to church tonight."

"Naw, mommy good since Ife came through with the rent money."

"I was wondering why she was down there frying chicken," Mystro joked. "But, what you gotta do for Ife to return the favor?"

"I'll worry about that shit later, we gonna party tonight," Native said. "Man, I ain't gonna lie, I was shook when shawty started screaming." She continued referring to the failed robbery attempt. "But you were quick on your feet by snatching me into that cut between the buildings, then running 'round the block. I'da never thought of that shit," Native confessed.

"Yeah, well I think it's safe to say we have no future in robbing to get rich. I'm pissed I even thought it was gonna fly." Mystro admitted embarrassed that she went along with the idea. "Here, take my picture." Mystro said handing Native her black iPhone, while she remained on the toilet.

"What's this for your flickgram page?" Native questioned while squaring up the phone to get the perfect angle from her position on the toilet seat.

"Naw, you know I gotta take a picture of what I wear so I can avoid repeats," Mystro explained. "How you think I was able to put this fit together?"

"I forgot you be on that shit."

Mystro refused to be caught wearing the same thing out in public. To avoid it, she took pictures of her outfits and texted them to herself to keep accurate records of what she wore, and the date she wore it. She practiced this ritual every time she left the house.

"Alright, get ready," Native said.

Mystro stood still and allowed Native to capture the moment. "Don't forget the shoes," she instructed.

Native sucked her teeth, and snapped a quick picture of Mystro's entire ensemble. Including her all black foamposites.

"Here," Native handed her phone back. "I'm 'bout to jump in this shower so I can get dressed too. That mothafuckin' club gonna be packed tonight," Native continued as she flushed the toilet, and closed the bathroom door.

* * * 2 **HOURS LATER** * * *

The club was dark and moist. It was crammed wall to wall with D.C.'s finest, and not so finest lesbians. PRIDE weekend meant everyone who was gay, and in the know, was out in the city partying. Mystro and Native chose to ring in their party weekend at a club called, "The Delta".

The two twenty-something friends posted up against a wall, both drinking Corona after Corona in an attempt to rid their thoughts of their crazy day.

As attention-starving-bucket-head's continuously walked back and fourth in front of the duo, Mystro looked over each one, carefully searching for who could become Mrs. Mason. But in this room, nobody caught her eye. Native wasn't interested in the girls' antics either, she was too concerned with figuring out where her next dollar would come from. They attempted to discuss their financial problems over the club's loud music.

"Son, I know I keep bringing it up, but what the fuck we gonna do 'bout some ends?" Native questioned. "I can't keep hitting Ife up for no bread. She too freaked out, and my payback's gonna be wild." Native yelled referring to the fact that she would have to perform crazy sexual acts in luei of the money Ife gave her.

C. WASH

Shrugging her shoulders and taking another sip of beer, Mystro laughed then yelled, "I guess we gotta look for another job, it shouldn't be that hard to find one."

"Get the fuck outta here. No, I'm not 'bout to go begging for no job. I can't do it. I'd rather get a pack and sell it on the block."

"Get a pack of what," Mystro shot back. "You ain't no dealer, fake ass corner boy." Mystro laughed adjusting her black frame personality glasses.

"Fuck you, moe. We probably get cracked as soon as we hit the block fucking with your scary ass anyway," Native came back at her.

"What up ladies?" The MC shouted through the microphone from the stage. She was addressing the excited crowd of women. "I hope you got your cash on deck cuz the show getting ready to jump off tonight," she screamed, and the crowd got hype.

Mystro and Native watched as most of the women in the club rushed toward the stage in anticipation.

"Aight, we switching it up on you early," MC advised. "Up first is one of my niggas making her debut tonight, so be good to her. Without further delay, I give you, *Hardcore*." When the MC walked away, the DJ dropped Trey Songz's track, *Love Faces*.

"When the fuck they start allowing Dom's to dance first?" Mystro asked disgusted.

Native shrugged her shoulders unable to answer her question. "I guess good talent is hard to come by."

They both looked on as the Dom strutted onto the stage, over emphasizing every slouch-socked-black timberland step she made, to the words of the song.

The scene was too much for Mystro and Native, who were normally uninterested in watching Dom ladies perform. But it wasn't the Dom's performance so much as the crowd's reaction that they paid close attention to. The women seemed to love the mess on the stage. Especially a silver-haired fox, that stood directly in front of Timbo Dom, spewing out bills like a broken ATM machine. She must have thrown at least fifty dollars in ones at her boots. While several other women who could not get enough, joined the older admirer.

"Now this is what we need to be doing," Native shouted with nothing but dollars signs in her eyes.

Mystro looked at Native like she was crazy, and laughed her out. It was no way Native would be able to convince her to do anything like dancing half naked in front of an entire club of people.

From the corner the room, Mystro noticed that she too had an admirer. And she seemed to be approaching the two friends.

She made her way right up to Mystro, and stood so close she could have kissed her. Mystro felt weird and not sure what the woman wanted, but took it upon herself to bend down and allow her to whisper in her ear.

"Your fine ass needs to be up there on that stage," the admirer told her, "and I'd gladly pay to see it too." She finished, as she tucked a fifty-dollar bill into the collar of Mystro's black Hugo Boss Polo shirt, before stepping off.

# CHAPTER 6

It had been a couple weeks since Mystro and Native were at the club celebrating gay pride weekend. Mystro had gone on a few job interviews, but was still unemployed and it began to weigh on her heavily. Native was adamant about them trying the dance routine out at the club for money. She used each and every moment they were together as an opportunity to convince Mystro to do it, until she gave in. And after much debate, argument and deliberation, Mystro caved.

The night of their first performance finally arrived. They were at the Delta Nightclub, and it was packed. Although it was not as cramped as it was two weeks ago during PRIDE, the crowd was nice. The club walls were just as sweaty as ever, as the ladies of the rainbow partied on the upper and lower floors within the club. In less than one hour, Mystro and Native would make their debut. While women of all shapes and ages paid the ten-dollar cover charge for admission, Mystro and Native prepared in the dressing room downstairs.

"Slim, you need to come over here, hit this bob and relax." Native said.

"I'm good, champ. I gave you my word, so I know this shit gotta go down. I'm 'bout to take a few shots and I'll be ready." Mystro advised.

"Shit, well let's get it in." Native yelled excited."

"Hook me up a shot too, Fam," Baby Dom chimed in.

Mystro cut her eyes toward Baby Dom, acknowledging her statement, but completely ignoring her request. Instead she poured out two shots of peach Ciroc in two plastic cups, and handed one to Native.

"Ain't no turning back at this point," Mystro stated, "it's now or never." She dropped her shot back in one gulp.

Native followed suit, and effortlessly downed her shot also. There was a knock at their door. "Ya'll up next," the club MC opened the door and shouted. She closed the door promptly after her statement was made.

"Damn, that was quick. Here take another shot, Native," Mystro instructed.

"What about my cup? I need some confidence too," Baby Dom pleaded.

"BD, you not fucking dancing. You just collecting our money. Fuck you need a shot for?" Mystro asked.

"Man, I'm nervous. If ya'll embarrass ya'll self up there, I'ma feel that shit too from the crowd, feel me?" Baby Dom advised.

"Your nineteen-year-old-young-ass ain't 'bout to get drunk in here on my watch. It's one thing if we drinking a beer while kicking it on the porch 'round the way, but I'm not fucking with you and no liquor out in these streets. No, sir." Native said, shutting her down.

"Exactly, plus I need you to make sure you concentrate on our paper," Mystro stated. "Collect it and put it in your pocket. Then after our set, meet us back down here with our cash in hand. *ALL* of it, not some, you got me?" Mystro continued.

"Oh you got me all wrong, Fam. I wouldn't take ya'll money. Of course, I got you," Baby Dom shouted, with a crazy twitch in her right eye.

Mystro gave her a serious look. "I'm not playing with you. We not doing this shit for free. Get our money and come back here."

"Time waits for no one, let's hit it," Native said breaking her stare, as she put out her blunt and headed toward the door.

The duo both checked how they looked in the mirror before exiting the small dressing room. As they approached the staircase leading to the floor stage upstairs, Mystro noticed how a few of the femmes rushed up behind them. They were coming to see the show, since they knew they were about to perform.

Mystro's stomach flipped with nervousness. She noticed the smile on Baby Dom's face, as she followed behind them too. Baby Dom thought them dancing was hilarious, and couldn't wait to see it go down.

As they approached the area close to the stage, they checked themselves one more time. Mystro smoothed out her black Levi's jeans. She made sure her black button down shirt hung open just right, revealing her white wife beater underneath.

Native ran her hands through her bone straight hair, and carefully adjusted her red Washington Nationals cap securely on her head. She flipped the collar of her black polo shirt, and made sure all except the top button was closed.

While they were getting ready, the femme dancer on the stage wrapped up her set. When she was done, the MC grabbed the mic to announce Mystro and Native's upcoming performance.

Mystro looked at Native, and raised her arm up, to give her a fist bump. Then, she threw on her shades and headed to the stage as the DJ played R. Kelley's, *Strip For You*.

As soon as the women in the crowd saw Mystro and Native ease onto the floor, they let out a thunderous yell. If they backed that reaction up with money, Mystro and Native stood to make bank.

However, although they were attractive, they did not have their act together. Since they were dancing as a team, they needed to be performing as one too. Instead, they had on two different outfits and they did not have a good dance routine. They were out there winging it.

Despite the half ass performance, some women still threw money at them. Especially an extra-large, extra-greasy, extra-old ass Dom lady. She was the type of Dom that could confuse someone. She was tall and big, and wore jeans and timbs, but had on a pink blouse and her hair was hard curled. The broad was on the fence between ugly-Femme and ugly-Dom. They referred to her as Biggie Dom, since she closely resembled a confused Biggie Smalls.

Mystro and Native completed the song, and the DJ put on a faster one. Baby Dom was on her job while they were on the stage. She collected any bills that hit the floor, and a few others that the femme who danced before them left behind.

Mystro and Native danced around to each woman that tipped them to express their gratitude, just as they observed many performers do. This inevitably meant that they had to thank Biggie Dom. It was clear that Mystro and Native did not want to approach her, but they had no choice. She tipped them most of the money they took in, so to slight her would be bad business.

As luck would have it, the song ended before they had to face Biggie Dom. They rushed off the stage, and hit it back to the dressing room, to avoid the mob. Mystro did not like the look in Biggie Dom's eyes. Her eyes screamed "PYCHO", so the two got the hell outta there, hoping she would not follow them.

"Oh my God. We really just did that shit," Native yelled, busting into the dressing room.

"I can't believe it either, son," Mystro said closing the door. "That shit felt so crazy."

"How much you think we made?" Native asked just as there was a light knock on the door.

"Oh shit," Mystro said looking at the closed door. "I'm not opening that shit. It might be that fake dom lady outside. I can't take no more of her, moe," She continued, staying away from the door.

After five minutes, the knocking stopped. Mystro decided to open the door slowly to see if the coast was clear. There was no psycho, but there was a gorgeous female waiting on the other side. Mystro was stuck when she saw her face, and Native rushed to the door to see what was happening.

"Come in," Native told the lady.

Mystro was still speechless. The woman's beauty was unmeasured.

Native and the female held a brief conversation, while Mystro looked on in silence. She was experiencing love at first sight, and was oblivious to what was being said.

*'DAMN, shawty is sexy as shit. God has finally answered my prayers. This is going to be my new wife.'* Mystro was deep in thought.

"My, this is Church," Native said trying to snap her friend out of the stupor. "Slim, you hear me?" Native asked, elbowing Mystro to the ribs.

She immediately snapped out of thought. She grabbed her side and mean mugged Native. "Why you do that, son? I heard you."

"Then say something," Native barked. "We have a guest."

"Hello, Mystro," Church said. "It's a pleasure to meet you." The female extended her petite hand toward her.

She grabbed Church's hand, and kissed the back, "Pleasure's all mine," She replied, in her best Billie Dee impersonation.

Church blushed.

Native gagged.

"Did you enjoy our show?" Mystro asked.

"Dog, she just said all that," Native chimed in. "I thought you was listening. She just said she caught our show, and thought it was cool but she can give us a few pointers if we interested." Native explained.

Church smiled, staring up at Mystro seductively.

Mystro was beyond embarrassed, but she pulled it together. "Forgive me, I had a few too many shots before the show," she replied. "What were you saying again?"

"It's ok, I was saying that I really enjoyed you guys up there, and I could tell the ladies did too. Especially one in particular." Church continued laughing. "Your friend referred to her as Biggie Dom I think."

"Yeah, I don't ever want to see that monster again," Native added. "I don't care how much money she spending."

"That's what I came to talk to you about," Church said. "She is exactly the type of admirer you play into. I think you guys have potential and if you allow me to work with you, I believe you can make major money.

Before Mystro responded, she looked out of the open door and noticed a female rushing down the steps toward her friends. She began yelling excitedly, "Some cute little Dom upstairs buying rounds for everybody. You better get one while they last!"

"Fuck, where is Baby Dom?" Mystro yelled.

# CHAPTER 7

Mystro and Native decided to take Church up on her offer to give them a few pointers for their show. They agreed to meet her at her home uptown, better known as Northwest DC. However, they were not prepared for what Church had in store.

They were all in Church's basement, as she positioned her five foot three inched frame directly in front of her ceiling to floor length mirror. She went over the dance routine that she choreographed for Mystro and Native. Even in her red leotard, fishnet stockings and red stilettos, she pulled off the masculine moves with the finesse of an Alvin Ailey dancer.

Church turned her small home's basement into a dance studio, complete with hardwood floors and mirrors. It had been a long time dream of her's to be a dancer, and she practiced hard on her art. But, until that dream was attained, she just taught those who were interested in what she learned on her own, and that included strippers.

"Mystro, what are you doing?" Church asked, looking at Mystro's reflection behind her in the mirror.

"Huh," Mystro replied, snapping out of her stare-fest. "What you mean what am I doing?"

"I'm going over the movements, and I see you looking but not dancing. Do you have your part?" Church asked, while approaching her iPod to pause the music. "The fuck is you giving, son?" Native asked Mystro. Native was out of breath, while doubled over with her hands on her knees. She used this moment to take a quick break. "We supposed to be working."

"What are ya'll talking about," Mystro questioned. "I'm dancing."

"No, you were watching," Church stated. "And, Native, what are you doing, sweetie? Do you think you have it?" Church continued. "Because from what I see you don't."

"Baby girl, don't even come for me," Native shot back. "I ain't even know we was coming over this joint to get all sweaty and shit. I woulda threw on more appropriate clothing if that was the case."

"That's my fault. When I gave you my information at the club, I should have been more specific about what we would be doing tonight," Church apologized. "I guess I didn't want to scare you off before you had a chance to see what I was talking about. But this is serious. You two are on stage as a team. So you already have an advantage on the rest of the Dom's. But, the big difference between you and them will be what you do in your performance," Church continued. "And how you move."

"What you mean?" Native asked. She dropped to the floor, and rolled over on her back, to catch her breath.

Mystro looked on in silence concentrating only on Church.

"What I mean is you have to cater to the women in the crowd. You have to mind fuck them so hard that they are willing to give their whole life, just for the possibility to gain your attention. To achieve this, your stamina has to be up, and you have to get this routine down."

"I'm not the one you need to be schooling." Native pulled herself to her feet. "Mystro, are you with me or are you out lunching?" She asked her friend.

"I'm with you," Mystro replied. "Fuck you talking about?"

"I'm saying, you ain't did shit but stare at this bitch's ass the whole time we been in here," Native responded angrily.

"Bitch," Church frowned.

"My bad, baby girl, I ain't mean no disrespect," Native stated. "I'm just saying, Mystro, if you wanna get with shawty, holla at me, moe. I'll get out ya'll way. But I thought this shit was for us to get right, and for us to get some paper. But, you in here bull-shitting. I mean I ain't no dancer, but at least I'm try-ing."

"Bullshitting," Mystro asked, leaning in. "Church, run that music from the beginning." Mystro requested.

Church dashed toward her iPod touch, and hit the play button. The base crawled through the speakers in the corners of the wall. Mystro immediately broke out in her routine. She used Church as her focus. Every move she made, was to seduce. While the performance went on, not only did Mystro prove that she had her routine down, but she also succeeded in tempting Church. She was highly impressed.

When the routine was over Mystro asked, "Now, what you goin' do, Native?"

Native looked on in disbelief. Her friend appeared stuck but she was actually focused.

"Man, fuck this," Native barked. "All this shit dumb anyway." Really she was just frustrated and unsure of her own part.

"Listen, I'm just trying to help ya'll get more money," Church explained. "But in order to do that, you have to listen to what I'm saying and do everything I ask." Her voice elevated. "The first thing I think we need to do is get in the gym, on the cardio machines, to get your stamina up." She wrapped her hand around her neat ponytail, and pulled it back.

"Hold up, hold up, I ain't training for the Olympics," Native said. "This shit is just to dance in front of a bunch of horny ass dykes. Ya'll got me fucked up if you think it's more than that."

"So what you saying, son, you not gonna do the shit?" Mystro asked.

"That's just what I'm saying. I'm gone." Native trudged up the basement steps, and out the front door.

Mystro walked toward the steps. "Native...Native," Mystro called out. "Come back, slim." The door closed.

"I'm sorry about my friend, Church. I really do appreciate you taking the time to help us out." Mystro turned away from the steps, and walked back towards Church.

She faced Mystro and Mystro noticed the sultry look in her eyes. It appeared as if Church was flirting with her all of a sudden.

Church could feel that Mystro was attracted to her, and she used this to her advantage.

Mystro watched as Church glided toward her. She admired her ample breasts and small waist. Even though Church was stacked, her movements were fluid. Everything she did was graceful and dainty. She was driving Mystro insane inside, and out. But, Mystro tried her hardest to maintain her cool; although she wanted nothing more than to marry her and run off into the sunset to build a family.

Church reached Mystro and cozied up close to her body. She looked up into Mystro's eyes and before she spoke, she used her index finger to run down Mystro's neck and collarbone. Then Church said, "I do not mind helping ya'll. Besides, the more time I spend with you, the better for me. But, I offered my assistance because I saw the potential in both of you. I'm looking to coach a team. So I need Native."

Mystro rolled her eyes upward. She knew how stubborn Native could be and was not looking forward to tackling this issue with her.

Church reached up and caressed Mystro's chin. "Get Native on board," She said. "And, trust me, it'll be worth it." She placed a soft kiss on Mystro's lips.

As far as Mystro was concerned, enough was said and she was in love, again.

# CHAPTER 8

"I ain't think you was gonna call me, Native," Ife said as Native kissed her stomach.

"Of course I called, I still owe you don't I? Now shut up and let me pay my debt," Native ordered.

When Native stormed out of Church's house like a spoiled two year old, she realized that she rode over there with Mystro, who was still inside the house. So how was she going to get home? Luckily she knew the neighborhood, and decided to walk to the end of the block to go to the 7-11. As she strutted down the street, she remembered one of her slide's (a girl she fucked without commitment), lived on the next street over.

Ife was an African girl who Native met in a reggae club a year ago. She never did much with her outside of sex, and that was fine with Native. Besides, Ife wasn't Native's type. Although she was a sexy chick with a natural and Afro centric look about her, she was too wild and demanding. She wore her hair in sister locks, and she always smelled of Egyptian musk or Coco butter. Although Native didn't like kicking it with Ife often, the sex was always good.

She called Ife and told her she was stuck around the corner. And fifteen minutes later, she pulled up on Native, and took her home. Now she was about to fuck.

Native continued to kiss Ife's stomach and inner thigh, making her way to her waiting clean shaved pussy. A bald pussy was a turn on to Native. She preferred her boxes that way.

She parted Ife's pussy lips with her tongue and her extra large clit popped out, the moment it was exposed. Native had a theory and method on eating pussy. She based her theory on the size of the girl's clit. She had to put in major work on the smaller hidden love buttons, but for the bigger ones, it was about consistency.

For Ife, she loved when Native used her tongue like a sharp dagger, and jabbed it in and out of her opening. She was driven to shear ecstasy when Native would tongue fuck her, and occasionally run her tongue over her clit. She was simple to bring to an orgasm and Native loved that the most, but she could never get enough and that was a problem.

"Oh...oh...shiiiiitttt," Ife yelled. "I'm cumming."

Native bore down harder, and sucked on Ife's clit, making sure she came fast and hard. She did.

Native lifted her head up, with her chin glistening. She used the inside of her black T-shirt's collar to wipe her mouth off. "Turn over," Native ordered

Ife onto her stomach. She knew she wasn't finished putting in work.

Ife happily obliged. She loved what was coming. This was the part of their sex game that she lived for.

Native positioned herself behind Ife in true doggie style formation. She pushed Ife's back down and commanded, "Ass up, girl."

Ife complied as she grabbed a pillow, and arched her back to position her ass in the air. Native pushed into her awaiting pussy, while on her knees. She pulled Ife's phat ass open wider with a hand on both her left and right cheek. She needed to expose Ife's pussy completely, so she could lean in and align their boxes like connect the dots.

When they were in sync, Native begin to grind her own clit against Ife's opening. Ife was a pro at this shit. She was able to use her intact kegel muscles to grab hold of Natives clit as if it was a dick. The squeezing of Native's clit drove her crazy.

The two continued to grind and fuck each other's brains out, until Native could no longer take anymore.

"Ahhhhhhh…fuck," Native screamed as Ife continued to whine her ass repeatedly to make Native cum hard.

As Native came Ife jumped up and got underneath her to suck her clit. She loved the way Native's cum tasted, and wanted to lap up all of her juices. This only sent Native into overdrive. She came again, harder, afterwards trying to push Ife off of her body.

"Stop," Native shouted. "You know I can't take all that shit." She was satisfied, and she wanted the game over. Native rolled off her knees and onto her back out of breath.

"I know, but I'm ready for round two," Ife whispered, as she jumped up and straddled Native's face.

Native was irritated but pushed through. She immediately gripped Ife's ass cheeks, and went back to work feasting on her saturated pussy.

"Mmmmm…ahhhhh…mmmm, damn you Indian looking mothafucka. That shit feels so good," Ife cooed.

Native hated when bitches talked shit to her. She liked for her females to have a little spice, and a smartass mouth occasionally, but in the bedroom, she was king. Ife popping off at the chops only made Native speed up her movements to make her bust quicker.

"Ahhh, oh shit. I'm cumming," Ife screamed, as she gripped Native's hair and rode her tongue while squeezing out her second orgasm. When completely finished, she scooted her body down and tried to lie on top of Native.

"Damn, ma, you was 'bout to drown me," Native said as she pushed Ife off of her body completely.

"What the fuck you expect? You ate this pussy down," Ife confessed as she rolled over onto her side.

"So, what you 'bout to do?" Native asked, standing up to grab her black Polo robe. She also grabbed her towel to wipe her face.

Ife sucked her teeth and said, "What you mean? I'm about to go to sleep."

"Not here you ain't. I gotta get up early tomorrow." Native lied.

Ife sucked her teeth even louder. "That's why you get the fuck on my nerves," she shouted. "I don't know when I'ma learn my fucking lesson." Ife scanned the room for her dress.

"Come on, boo, you knew what it was before you even came in here," Native explained. "I appreciate you looking out for me with the ride." Native continued handing Ife a towel. "But now its time for you to bounce."

"Oh so now you being a gentleman and handing me a towel to shower with?" Ife asked.

"Naw, ma, you can't take no shower. My mom's would lose it, she probably already 'bout to go on me cuz you in here screaming and shit," Native advised. "Use the towel to wipe up and then toss it over there in the hamper."

"This some bullshit. I'd be a dumb bitch if I ever came over here again," Ife stated, as she grabbed her knockoff Louis Vuitton bag. She located her dress and threw it over her naked body, stuffing her thong and bra inside her purse and before she headed towards the bedroom door she said, "Next time you need money or you stuck uptown, don't call me."

"Yeah aight. Hold up, shawty," Native stopped Ife. "Let me make sure the coast clear." Native moved past her towards the door.

She opened her bedroom door slowly, and peeked into the hallway. She saw her mother's bedroom door closed. She could see the TV light from the bottom of the door, and figured she was asleep. But before having Ife come out the room, she wanted to investigate why the dining room light was on downstairs. She walked down the steps to see who was in there.

She found Mystro standing in the dining room hanging up the house phone. She wore a look of anger and sadness on her face.

"Oh, what's up, slim. I ain't know you was home yet, what's wrong?" Native asked.

"Just finished talking to Mack, I gotta get up there to see him soon." Mystro said referring to her father.

"How he doing?" Native asked concerned. Mystro didn't say anything she just shook her head and looked towards the television in the living room. "Ok." Native said picking up the fact that Mystro didn't want to talk about it. "Is mommy down here?"

"Naw, I think she up there sleep." Mystro stated.

"Cool," Native responded. "Ife," she whispered loudly up the stairs. "Come down."

Ife came tip toeing down the stairs heated and walked right past Native who rested at the foot of the staircase.

Mystro noticed the tight lip on Ife, and chuckled under her breath as she got up and made her way to the door to unlock it.

"Bye, Mystro," Ife angrily shouted, ignoring Native. She walked passed Mystro and out the door.

"Aight, Ife," Mystro replied back, noticing that Baby Dom was running up the steps and towards the house.

"Before you kick me off the porch, here," Baby Dom said shoving a $20 dollar bill in Mystro's direction. "I know I owe ya'll $200 from tricking off the Delta bitches, but take this $20 and I'll only owe $180," Baby Dom said enthusiastically.

"Slim, give me that," Mystro said laughing, and snatching the money at the same time. "Walk Ife to the car." She ordered.

"Aight, Fam. I got you," Baby Dom said, as she followed behind the still fuming Ife.

After Mystro watched Ife get into the car, and Baby Dom trot off back down the block, she closed and locked the wooden storm door.

Native made her way to the couch, and threw her feet, dressed in her Washington Redskins slippers, onto the footrest in the living room.

"Son, can you believe Baby Dom lil ass?" Mystro asked, as she made her way to the couch to sit down.

"Yeah, I can believe her. And I know she better come up with the rest of our money too," Native said angrily.

"That was on us," Mystro admitted. "Baby Dom will always do what she does. We ain't have no business putting her on the money."

Native nodded her head. "You want to talk about Mack?"

"Not really, I think he running out of time and I just need to get up there and see him. But you know I hate doing that." Mystro confessed.

"You know I can go with you, slim. Just say the word."

Mystro nodded her head, appreciating her friend's support. "Hey, why you get in your feelings about Church and the routine?" She asked taking the subject off her dying father.

"Man, I ain't 'bout to do that choreographed shit. I can't believe you wanna do it either. Personally, I think shawty trying to get hooked into us for the loot. You better watch her too, she bossy as shit, son," Native stated.

"Naw, man, I don't think she's like that at all. I mean yeah, she seems like she serious about this routine, but I think that's only to make us sharper."

"Oh, really, and what she gonna get out of it?" Native asked sternly.

"I think she sweet on me, so she prolly just really wanna help us out. I don't think she want nothing."

"Sweet on you or not, people don't do something for nothing, remember that. Plus, you can't be going all in for every broad that got a phat ass and smile in your face. That's how you be getting caught up and if you not careful, you gonna be right back in that judge's courtroom." Native informed.

Mystro dismissed the courtroom statement. "I think you wrong 'bout her, Native. I really think she's the one. I can't explain it. But it's a feeling that I get when I'm around her. I think this woman is gonna change my life." Mystro confessed.

Native shook her head in disbelief of her best friends gullibility when it came to women. But before she could respond, Margret opened her bedroom door and shouted, "What smells like pussy and Shea butter in this mothafucka?"

# CHAPTER 9

"I'm already impressed," Church proclaimed as she stepped out of her custom made black BMW 650i.

"Impressed...why?" Mystro asked walking up to Church, and grabbing her gym bag from her. Mystro was a gentle-Dom if nothing else.

It was late in the evening, but Church suggested that Mystro meet her at the local gym. Church needed to help Mystro get her endurance up for her performance. She wanted both Mystro and Native to attend the sessions, but after their last meet, she knew it would take more convincing for Native to partake in the events.

"I'm impressed, because you actually showed up. I would've thought you were gonna fake on me," Church explained.

"Naw, I ain't scared of the gym, shawty," Mystro boasted.

"The gym ain't what you need to fear, boo," Church said. "It's this workout I'm 'bout to run you through." She walked through the door being held open for her by Mystro and winked.

The two checked in at the front desk, and proceeded to pick out a locker to temporarily secure their bags while they exercised. Mystro handed

Church her gym bag, while she pulled open a locker to make sure it was empty.

"Alright, mighty Mystro, quit stalling. Throw that stuff in there and meet me on the ARC trainer's," she instructed.

Mystro laughed her out, as she put on her black weight lifting gloves. Moments later, they stood parallel on their own ARC trainer cardio machines.

"Press manual, and put in your weight and thirty minutes time, and let's get started," Church coached. "But make sure your resistance is up to at least thirty," Church continued. "We not fucking around on these machines. We getting busy today."

"I gotchu," Mystro followed.

The duo got into the rhythm of the workout for the first ten minutes, until Mystro broke the silence. "So, what else do you do besides dance?" Mystro asked.

"Dancing is my passion, and I use my passion to help pay the bills," Church started. "But, it ain't enough so that's why I see our little situation as a good investment."

"Investment?" Mystro asked not sure of what Church was saying.

"Yes, when I'm finished with you two, you will be making money hand over fist. I figured I could take a small percentage of the profit in return for my guidance."

Mystro thought about what Native said. Although she may have been right about Church wanting something for her help, Mystro figured that she deserved to be paid; especially if Church's new routine made them a lot more money.

"I know you jive explained it already, but I'm still not clear on how exercising is gonna get me," Mystro paused. "I mean us, get paid." Mystro wiped a thin layer of sweat from her forehead with her towel.

"It's simple," Church started. "Have you ever been in a male strip club and seen them perform?"

Before answering the question, Mystro scanned her immediate surroundings to see if anyone was ear hustling. "Fuck no," she yelled, no longer caring who was listening. "Why you ask me that?"

"Because," Church laughed, "if you had seen a male stripper's performance you would know that they make a killing. Them mammas in there make sure they pay them dudes. I mean it's so serious, that some of them niggas have regular customers who basically tip so much they pay rent and car notes," Church advised.

"I bet. Them bamma's be out there butt ass, wit' they package jumping out in broads faces," Mystro frowned. "We ain't getting it in like that, shawty." Mystro gulped down her fruit punch Gatorade. "We got our limits."

"I don't expect you too, but them nigga's get paid because they sell the fantasy." Church wiped sweat from her forehead for the first time. "They wear costumes, and have routines. They do push-ups over top of women, and in between their legs. That takes stamina. Them women eat that shit up. It ain't all about being naked, it's about being creative."

"Creative huh…Like what?"

"Like pick your songs carefully. Your music should be seductive. You want them broads to start geeking the moment they hear the intro."

"Aight…I agree. I think we can handle that. What…else?" Mystro asked, out of breath from the intensity of her workout.

"Pick some fly outfits. And if you gonna wear shorts or strip down to boxers," she looked at Mystro's legs, "please make sure you oil them knee-caps."

Mystro stutter stepped and almost fell off the machine embarrassed by Church's last statement. "Damn, slim, you going," she laughed. "Yeah, ok maybe I can have you oil a nigga up before I hit the stage. How that sound?" Mystro continued to laugh.

"Oh, I can handle that, boo, it would be my pleasure," Church flirted.

Mystro grabbed at her almost empty Gatorade bottle to finish it off, in an attempt to hide her blushing. She always got a little embarrassed when women openly flirted with her.

"So you think we'll pull in bigger bank if we add them tweaks to our routine and get our stamina up?" Mystro asked changing the subject back.

"I guarantee it," Church shouted, "No offense, but ya'll came out there like some inexperienced thugs bopping around. You have to be different then the thugs they've seen, you all must be gentlemen."

"Man, all this shit over my head for real. I'm just doing this because Native convinced me to and I gave her my word I would. She knew I wanted to make a quick come up, so I can get my own place." Mystro confessed.

"I hear you, ya'll want to move out of the house and on your own, huh?"

"No, I'm moving out, Native still gonna be staying at home. I need to build my foundation so I can start my family." Mystro stated looking Church dead in her eyes.

Church smiled and changed the subject. "So do you think Native will get on board with my plan?" she asked.

"Man, I don't know. She don't even be wanting to talk about it. I think she feels like its too much work and she was on doing some simple shit to get the money."

Church remained silent. She turned away from Mystro and stared directly out in front of her machine. She needed a plan. The cardio machines switched their workout to cool down mode, which made Mystro happy. She was beyond winded.

"I told you I would work that ass didn't I?" Church taunted, snapping out of her daydream.

"You got it, ma," she conceded, while wiping her whole head with her towel.

As Mystro looked around, she noticed that the once semi-full gym only had a few people left. "Oh, shit…We shut this joint down. It's time to go," she stated hopping off the cardio machine.

"Don't worry, I'm locking up tonight," Church said hopping off her arc trainer as well and walking up to the front desk.

Mystro observed as Church spoke to the person who checked them in just thirty-five minutes ago. After only a few minutes, the person left the gym along with the few remaining patrons. Church locked the door, and turned down some of the lights.

"So, Mystro…can you swim?" Church asked, as she walked up to Mystro grabbing her hand and leading her into the locker room.

* * * POOL * * *

Church led Mystro through the locker room, and out to the pool deck. All the lights were out on the deck except for the indigo bulbs that illuminated the heated pool water. Mystro stood near the shallow end taking in her surroundings. The water was beautiful. As she stared at the calmness of the pool, she was pulled out of her gaze by the sound of Xscape's song, *Softest Place On Earth.* The music began to flow out and take over the deck.

Church, who briefly disappeared, walked back into Mystro's sight completely naked. Mystro's heart rate sped up and her stomach fluttered when she saw how sexy Church looked. Her ponytail was lost as her hair now gently teased her shoulders as she bounced toward the deep end. Mystro noticed what appeared to be a tattoo on Church's right thigh. It was fairly big, but it was too dim to make out what it was, from the distance the two had between them. As Church dove into the water, Mystro felt like someone glued her feet to the concrete.

"Are you gonna leave me in here all alone?" Church asked as she emerged from her dive and swam closer to her.

Mystro immediately sprung into action. Although she did not get completely nude, she stripped down to her sports bra and boxer briefs before jumping into the middle of the pool to meet Church.

"You are so sexy, Church," Mystro confessed looking deep into her eyes. "I been waiting for this since the moment I met you."

"I know," Church said staring directly up into Mystro's eyes while simultaneously placing her breasts up against the taller Mystro's stomach.

That did it for Mystro, normally she liked to take her time and court her women, but enough was enough. Clearly, Church wanted it and Mystro was ready to give it to her. She figured they could work out the details of what this meant for their relationship later.

Mystro reached under the water and gripped Church by her ass cheeks hoisting her up. Church followed suit by wrapping her legs around Mystro's waist. The two were now eye to eye and Church threw her arms around Mystro's neck.

Mystro leaned in and stole a passionate deep tongue kiss from Church, while slowly walking her to the edge of the pool wall. When they reached the wall, Mystro used her hands to explore all over Church's body. The two continued to kiss while Mystro slid her hand over Church's breasts, and down her stomach to her awaiting pussy. She used her index finger to slide inside Church. She could not believe how slick and wet she was. This boosted Mystro, she hoisted Church's body onto the edge of the pool and immediately took in her tattoo fully. It was of praying hands with a statement that read, *Church brings them to their knees*. It was a wrap; Mystro never had anyone this sexy in her life, not even Leslie could fuck with her.

Her mind wandered to thoughts of Leslie, but surprisingly, she did not get sad. She figured Leslie was taken out of her life to make room for her true soul mate, Church.

Now Mystro stared deeply into the eyes of the beautiful creature in front of her, and had a strong urge to devour her whole.

Mystro grabbed Church by her waist, and pulled her into another kiss before lifting Church back in the air, but this time, it was to place her pussy directly into her mouth. Church was in shock as Mystro worked her tongue, and lips all over her completely shaved pussy.

"Mystro…mmmm…this feels so good. Ohhhhh, baby please don't stop." Church stared down at Mystro and moaned while wrapping her hands around Mystro's neck. Her legs draped over her back.

Mystro did not comment, she was too busy on her quest to make Church stutter. She grabbed Church's ass cheeks, and sped up the motion of her tongue over Church's erect clit.

"Oh shit, Mystro…you gonna make me cum all over that tongue…fuckkkkkkkkk." She threw her head back and screamed, releasing her cum onto Mystro's tongue.

Mystro licked up every drop, before removing her tongue from inside of Church's soft spot. She put Church down into the pool water, and dropped her head under too, to rinse her face off.

There was a brief moment of silence. Mystro was on cloud nine, until she noticed that Church appeared to be in her head, and deep in thought.

She tried to walk out of the pool without looking at Mystro. But before she could, she grabbed her, pulling Church directly in front of her as she sat on the pool steps.

"Shawty, what's up? Why you looking all crazy and shit?" Mystro asked.

Church didn't say anything.

"Church," Mystro said, "What's wrong?"

Church turned towards Mystro and straddled her lap, while wrapping her arms back around her neck.

"Mystro, I really like you," she began. Mystro's heart beat quickened and her stomach fluttered. "I've been feeling you since day one, but it won't work." Church lowered her head.

"What you talking about, ma," Mystro asked confused. She knew the sex was right so what was the problem? "Why won't it work?"

"It won't work because you can't afford me. The only way it could possibly work is if we can work together." Church stared into Mystro's eyes, before placing a kiss on her lips. "But, working together means all three of us. So, if you want to be with me, you have to bring me Native." She finished.

Mystro was in a bind. She was already head over heels for Church but she was also loyal to her friend. She didn't want to create a problem between her and Native. But, she felt Church was everything she always wanted in a wife and knew she would be perfect to have a family with. She had no idea what to do.

Church leaned in and planted another passionate kiss on Mystro's lips.

It was settled, Mystro had to find a way to get Native back in the routine.

# CHAPTER 10

"It's all in how you hold the steel in your hand and where you put your eye," Mystro coached.

She was at the gun range in Timonium Maryland. There were many closer ranges, but she liked to take the hour plus drive from DC to practice her accuracy. Normally, the drive gave her some alone time to think. However, today, Native accompanied Mystro. She needed to somehow convince her to come back in the fold of their routine, under Church's guidance.

"Damn, moe, where you learn to shoot that shit on point like that?" Native asked, observing how precisely Mystro hit her mark every time.

"What," Mystro asked placing the black and silver Taurus .45 down and removing her earmuffs. "What you just say, son?" Mystro asked.

"I said how the fuck you know how to hit that target on point like that, you ain't no banger or no cop are you?" Native joked.

"Practice, man," Mystro stated. "You know I be coming out here all the time. What you think I was doing?" Mystro picked the gun back up and removed the clip.

"Nigga, off no bullshit, I thought you was coming out here for pussy and not telling me," Native said jokingly. "I know how secretive you be sometimes."

Mystro laughed at Native and continued to reload the clip with more practice rounds. She dug into her green khaki cargo shorts to grab more ammo. "Aight, son, it's your turn," Mystro informed. "Have you ever shot this type of tool before?"

"Yeah, every New Year's, when Uncle Bob was alive, we would shoot his joint up in the air, outside round the way," Native said. "You know that."

"You talking about the gun we used at the mall," Mystro questioned. "Cuz if you are that ain't no .45," Mystro schooled. "And as far as I knew, you never shot it before, so your answer should be no."

"Man, whatever, just hand it here," Native said attempting to grab the gun out of Mystro's grip.

"Hold up," Mystro yelled. "This shit ain't no toy, it got live rounds in here."

"Aight…aight, I'ma be careful," Native promised.

Native took the tool out of Mystro's hand carefully, and shot at the paper target but nothing happened.

"Son, cock the mothafucka…I know you ain't that green," Mystro teased.

"Nigga, I know that," Native shot back, "I just thought you did it for me."

Native used her left hand to pull back the slide on the gun. It slid back smoothly before Native released it, allowing it to spring back into its original state, successfully loading a round into the chamber.

"Now, don't just point and shoot, slim. Use the front sight to set up your shot," Mystro stated, pointing at the tip of the weapon before placing her earmuffs over her neatly braided cornrows, and back over her ears.

Mystro watched as Native shot all over the target wildly. She knew that making Native an excellent shot would not come anytime soon. So she decided to call it a day, before Native accidently hit the wrong shit and caught charges.

"Aight…aight, son," Mystro yelled trying to get Native to stop her wild ambush. "Stop shooting."

"What…why?" Native asked confused. "I'm killin' this shit."

"Yeah, that's the point," Mystro said taking the .45 out of Native's hand, and removing the clip, releasing the last remaining bullet in the chamber.

"You are horrible," Mystro teased. "How the hell you got a gun in the house and was gonna fake use it on someone, when you can't shoot for shit?"

"I never said I knew how to shoot, I just know how to act like I do. Plus, mommy vicious with that shit; don't let all the praying fool you. If something ever went down at the crib we good, she a crack shot." Native explained.

"Whatever...let's go grab some grub. All this gunfire in the air is making me jive hungry." Mystro said packing up the weaponry to turn back in to the gun range managers.

* * * **HOOTERS** * * *

"Slim, who the fuck you been calling? You blowing up the shit out somebody phone." Native asked observing the way that she repeatedly tried to reach someone on her cell phone.

Mystro did not respond right away. She continued to hit the button on her iPhone that read, "Wifey" in an attempt to call Church. "Don't worry 'bout who the fuck I'm calling, champ," Mystro replied defensively.

"I'm just saying, it can't be that serious. If they ain't answering maybe it's cuz they don't wanna talk, or they can't. Try texting 'em and see what happens," Native suggested, while grabbing her glass and throwing back the rest of her beer.

Mystro was beyond heated. She hated that there were times she tried to call Church, and could not reach her. She didn't care that the repeat calling may give Church the impression that she was a borderline stalker. She just wanted to get her on the phone.

"Fuck it," Mystro yelled, slamming her phone down on the table before grabbing her drink.

"Whoa, homie. You burnt up? Shawty musta finally threw that thing on your hopelessly in love ass and got you twisted." Native laughed, taking a bite out of her chicken wing. "I can't stand when you start checking for a broad. You really get to tripping. Why do you always go overboard with women?"

"What you talking about, I'm not even calling that girl." Mystro lied, attempting to conceal her anger. "I was trying to call the hospice about Mack but the line is busy."

"Don't lie to me, Mystro. You forget that I know you better than you know yourself." Native admitted.

Mystro was caught. Instead of continuing to lie, she sat in silence and tried to eat her food.

"Now I see why you ain't been home a lot lately. You prolly been stuck up under shawty like her shadow and shit." Native stated.

"Yeah, aight I admit, we been kicking it, but it ain't what you think," Mystro added. "I'm chilling right now."

"That's what you always say, son. Next thing I know you browsing jewelry stores looking for rings and shit." Native replied, before laughing hysterically.

"Shut the fuck up, son," Mystro said throwing a chicken bone across the booth in Native's direction.

"Go 'head, man. You 'bout to get a stain on my white Polo shit," Native yelled, dodging the flying foul bone.

"What difference do it make? You only wear your white T's once before tossing 'em or balling in 'em, anyway." Mystro said sarcastically.

The Hooters waitress came over to the booth, and placed the check on the table. Mystro grabbed it up before reaching into her cargo's to grab her wallet.

"Damn, the fuck you doing, slinging?" Native questioned, while eyeballing the two crisp one hundred dollar bills Mystro had in her black leather wallet.

"Naw, just cuz you wanted out doesn't mean I stopped performing," Mystro explained. "Church got me doing some small solo shit for practice up the spot. I'm not doing too bad for myself either." Mystro placed the cash into the Hooter's bill folder.

Native was silent. She thought about the amount of money she had in her own pocket, and felt like maybe another sit down with Church was in order. To be honest all she had to show for her stubbornness were a pair of brand new Lebron X's that she convinced Ife to cop for her. But, it wasn't like she could pay no bill with them either.

"It could be more of this for everybody if you come back in, son," Mystro said looking at Native in her attempt to plant her seed to have Native rejoin the group. "But I can't make you. The decision is yours."

Before Native could respond, a guy at the booth adjacent to Mystro and Native began coughing non-stop.

"Sir, are you alright?" The Hooters waitress asked him.

The guy continued to cough as if something went down his throat wrong until he suddenly threw-up all over his table. His stomach contents missed the waitress, but splattered slam on Native's brand new Lebron's. Her new shoes were ruined.

Native was furious. Without further pause or care about her reserved feelings towards Church, Native said, "Son, why don't you go 'head and call ole girl right now. Tell her I'm ready to play ball."

# ■ CHAPTER 11

From the open doorway, Mystro watched Church's every move as she instructed her Zumba class at the local gym. She was completely smitten with Church and thought she was mesmerizing. She continued to gawk at her from the hallway as Native looked on in pity.

"Son, I'm mad as shit that you bringing that girl roses," Native said angrily, standing next to her. They were waiting for the class to be over to have their meeting with Church. Mystro was intending on helping Native and Church make amends, in the hopes that they could get money together again. Her other aim was to make Church happy so she could give Mystro a chance.

"Mind your business, young." Mystro said growing tired of Native giving her unsolicited two cents about her and Church.

"I'm serious, you not gonna have to worry about me fucking this shit up," Native responded. "Shawty gonna run scared behind your stalking ass."

"Nigga, stop hating," Mystro shot back. "You need to be taking notes."

The class just finished and Mystro anxiously walked into the room before any of the dance students had a chance to exit.

"Hey, babe, did you miss me?" Mystro asked Church, handing her the rainbow colored roses, and leaning in for a kiss.

"Hey," Church replied, a little embarrassed, turning her head so Mystro kissed her cheek instead of her lips. "Thank you, you shouldn't have." She continued, noticing how some of her students looked on in shock before leaving the classroom.

"You welcome, ma, that's light work," Mystro said proudly not realizing Church was not as excited as she should have been.

"What's up stranger," Church said to Native, breaking the awkward moment.

"What up, girl," Native said, shaking her head at Mystro.

"So, you ready to work with me on this?" Church asked.

"Yeah, yeah…I guess so. I mean I saw the loot my nigga had and figured it was time to put my pride to the side for the greater good of my pockets." Native confessed.

"That's what I'm talking about," Church said while turning to face Mystro to wink.

Mystro blushed.

"So I see you fly again today, but I hope you brought some workout clothes. I gotta get you on them cardio machines." Church stated, referring to how Native was dressed.

"Naw, fuck all that," Native yelled. "I got my shit. Play me some music."

Mystro was in disbelief, and a little skeptical of what Native was about to do. She sat on the hardwood floor with her back up against the mirror to take a front row seat. Church walked over to her iPod to select a song for Native.

She selected, *Make A Movie*, by Twista and Chris Brown. The song was a bit faster than what they would normally dance off, but Native worked it out. She began her routine and executed every single move without fail. Mystro watched in shock as Native commanded her routine with accuracy. Church moved her body to the music and could not remove the smile off her face. She was pleased and impressed.

Mystro noticed how happy Church was. And not to be outdone, she jumped up from her floor seat and fell in line next to Native while contributing her part of the routine. They both finished out the performance and brought the dance to a close.

Church was elated. "Ok, I see someone been practicing."

"Told you I had my shit." Native answered.

"What about me, baby?" Mystro asked thirsty for attention.

"I know you had your part, hon. But you did look good together."

"So what's next, coach?" Native asked.

"I think class is over for the day," Church replied. "It's time to go look for outfits for you two. Ya'll trying to hit the mall?"

"Fuck yeah, shopping is my favorite hobby." Native boasted.

Mystro shook her head and laughed at her friend before walking towards Church. She waited for her to finish gathering her belongings and packing her gym bag. When she had it ready and zipped, Mystro picked it up off the table to carry it out to the car. Church grabbed her roses and smiled at Mystro.

Although Church knew Mystro overdid it when it came to her, she loved how sweet she was at times. No one had ever carried her things for her, ever. She loved her chivalry.

The three women walked out of the classroom and directly out of the crowded gym. Mystro held the door open as Church led them out into the parking lot. They were headed towards Church's ride, when a nigga in a gold Lexus jumped out of his car and stormed up to Church.

Mystro and Native both stopped in their tracks to observe the scene. The nigga grabbed Church by her right elbow and pulled her to him forcefully. In the friction, she dropped her roses.

Mystro went from zero to sixty in two seconds and rushed up to the dude with Native quickly on her Jordan heels. "What the fuck is up, slim?" Mystro yelled and pushed him from behind, while dropping

Church's gym bag and squaring her body up in preparation to go toe-to-toe.

Dude stumbled off the push but once he regained his footing, he turned around slowly to face Mystro with pure venom in his eyes.

The nigga was six feet tall, and looked like all muscle. Mystro may have gotten her crazy ass whooped all over the parking lot, but she wasn't gonna let some nigga manhandle her boo either. Native stood directly by Mystro's side with her fist balled up ready for whatever.

"Church, you better tell this wanna be nigga that I'm 'bout to treat her like the dude she thinks she is, and cave her fucking chest in." Dude said.

"I already made the first move, champ," Mystro yelled back. "Make yours."

# CHAPTER 12

It had been days since Mystro spoke to Church and she was losing her mind. She tried reaching her after the incident that happened in the gym's parking lot but Church never answered her calls. Mystro even showed up at Church's house unannounced to talk to her, but could never catch her home. She didn't want Native to know she was upset, so she had to keep her cool. And the day to show and prove finally arrived.

The club was dimly lit and the sexy older femme dancer, draped in her red sequined evening gown, made her final pleas for tips, before leaving the floor stage. The Delta was famous for allowing older women, who still had it, to grace the stage. Mystro and Native stood at the edge, as their time to shine was fast approaching. They dropped back two shots each of their favorite peach Ciroc until their liquid wings appeared.

"Time to put in work," Mystro yelled, holding up her fist out to Native.

"Showtime," Native yelled, back as she pounded Mystro's fist.

"Yes sir...that was Ms. Queen, give her some love." MC yelled into the microphone at the crowd. Queen, the older dancer, took her exit stage left walking right by Native but not before leaving her with a wink.

Native smiled and winked back.

Mystro laughed.

"Aight, ladies, the moment you've all been waiting for is upon us. Returning to our stage, new and improved, give it up for *Hersband Material*," she announced Mystro and Native's new stage name as they walked out.

The DJ played an instrumental version of their requested song, *Mirror*, by Neyo, as the spotlight rolled slowly up on Mystro and Native from foot to head. They appeared before the club donned in smoking jackets and silk pajama pants. Completing their look with ascots and leather fur lined slippers. Native's hair was parted down the middle and styled into her traditional French braids. Mystro's head no longer played host to her cornrows, her hair was blown out straight and hanging below her shoulders. Accompanying these two smooth Dom's on stage now was a full length, stand-alone mirror and a single chair that Baby Dom set up.

The ladies standing around the stage began to scream and whistle. They threw dollars on the stage although Mystro and Native hadn't made a move. The duo remained still all except their eyes. They appeared to be scanning the crowd before them. Both of their eyes settled on a short, thick, dark-skinned femme with slanted eyes. Mystro and Native looked at each other, shared a head nod and then looked back at the girl.

Mystro reached her hand out to the girl. The woman accepted her hand, and Mystro led her onto the floor stage. Once she was there, Native grabbed her waist and whispered into her ear, before Mystro led her to the chair directly in front of the mirror. The money continued to pour in as the spectators soaked up the show.

Mystro sat the lucky lady down, as Native stood in front of her blocking her reflection from the mirror. Native began to open her crimson jacket, revealing her ascot and wife beater. She untied the neck ware, and slipped it behind the girl's back. With one swift move Native pulled the girl up. Once she was on her feet, Mystro kicked the chair out from under her. Native pulled her in close to her body and began to eye fuck her. Just then, the DJ dropped the regular version of Neyo's ballad. The femme volunteer looked on in complete anticipation of their next move.

Biggie Dom, who is also in attendance, was in awe of the duo just as she had been before. Baby Dom is there and makes an attempt to start to collect all the fallen money, when Church comes out of nowhere and smacks her hand.

"Uh uhn…I got it," Church advised. "Go get a drink," she ordered. "I got this."

If looks could kill, Church would sure enough be a stiff. Baby Dom bounced off to the bar, but not before mean mugging Church.

After ten minutes of seduction, screams and flowing money. The duo wrapped up their elaborate show. The club went crazy and begged for more.

"Son, we banged that shit out," Native screamed the moment she burst through the dressing room door, leaving it open for Mystro.

"Yeah," Mystro said unenthused walking through the open door removing her ascot and jacket.

"What's the matter with you, nigga," Native asked taking off her slippers.

Mystro didn't answer; she turned her attention to Church followed by Baby Dom walking through the dressing room door.

"Oh my God, ya'll killed up there." Church yelled in excitement, running up to Mystro to give her a hug.

Mystro bent down and hugged Church, and immediately noticed the sour face that Baby Dom made over Church's shoulder.

"Look at all this money ya'll made," Church displayed. "It has to be at least a thousand dollars here, if not more and it's all yours, minus my twenty percent of course." Church continued.

"Mmm hmm, I knew you was gonna get yours somehow." Native commented sarcastically. "Here you go, young nigga. Take this ball, you paid back that debt so you earned this bump." Native told Baby Dom, while handing her a hundred dollars.

"Naw, Fam, I'm good," Baby Dom responded, in a sullen demeanor. "Look, I'ma wait for ya'll out by the ride." she finished before leaving out of the dressing room.

The room held an uncomfortable silence as all three women took in the unrecognizable mood Baby Dom was in.

"Uh, look, Native, do you mind if I speak with Mystro alone?" Church asked.

"Yeah, it's cool. I wanna go check on my youngin' anyway," Native stated. "I'll see you up-stairs, My." She continued, grabbing her things and leaving out the room, closing the door behind her.

"Mystro," Church started, "Why are you acting so distant? I thought you'd be excited to see me to-night."

"Where you been, Church, I haven't talked to you in days."

"Baby, I had to go to New York to teach a class of teenage girls. While I was out there, I lost my phone. You know how I have to go out of town eve-ry now and again. I told you that." She explained. "But you knew I would be here tonight, I missed you." She continued trying to pull Mystro in for a kiss.

Mystro kissed her, but still wore a look of concern on her face.

"What's wrong now?" Church asked.

"I'm still jive pissed about that nigga that manhandled you in the parking lot," Mystro confessed. "I don't know no landlord that be trying to fling folks around and shit. So something doesn't sound right."

"So you don't believe me? I told you he was pissed because I shorted the money for my rent since he didn't fix my hot water heater." Church explained.

"Yeah, I heard all that, but it still don't sit right. And truth be told, I ain't got room to be heated since you not officially mine anyway." Mystro stated sadly.

"Don't start this again."

"I told you, Church, I wanna be with you and hopping in and out of your bed every now and again ain't enough for me no more."

"And I told you that you have to be able to support me before I could even consider a relationship with you."

"What you call this," Mystro asked grabbing at the money they just made dancing. "I can take care of you, I will take the best care of you too." She pleaded.

Church looked up into Mystro's watering eyes and didn't respond.

"I want you to be mine and, I'm willing to do whatever you want to prove it." Mystro said. "Will you be my lady?"

# CHAPTER 13

Mystro, Native and Baby Dom were in *DC Tat's Tattoo Parlor* in the northwest section of Washington DC. Mystro and Native were preparing to add more artwork to their bodies. They believed a person could never have enough ink on them, especially if they held meaning.

"Hey, Fam, we should all get matching tat's," Baby Dom yelled over Native's shoulder, as she was having her own name put on her right wrist.

"Baby Dom, back your hype ass up," Native barked. "Ain't nobody 'bout to get no gay ass matching ink wit' you. Fuck outta here." She laughed.

"Yeah what you have in mind, Baby Dom, a rainbow and our initials in a pot of gold at the end?" Mystro clowned.

"Oh ya'll going…all I'm saying is we crew right? We should have matching tat's, feel me?" Baby Dom pled.

"That's cute, son, real touching. Maybe next time." Mystro said, handing the artist her credit card to pay for her work.

"Man, that's fucked up like shit," Baby Dom said, walking away from Native and towards where the artist was setting up for Mystro's tattoo.

Mystro took her black Polo T-shirt off revealing her black wife beater, and current tattoos on her arms. She pointed to the left side of her chest, where her new ink would be housed.

Baby Dom stood behind Mystro waiting for the artist to place the sketched tattoo in position on Mystro's chest. From the position in which she stood, Baby Dom could not see what the sketch looked like. Until Mystro sat in the chair and leaned back.

"Noooo…," Baby Dom screamed. "What you doing, Mystro," She asked, putting her hands on top of her mini locs that were twisted all over her head.

"Fuck is you yelling 'bout, BD," Native asked, while having her new completed tattoo bandaged up. After it was wrapped, Native got up and headed to where Mystro sat in preparation for her work. When she got there, she saw the outlined stencil of Mystro's tattoo. It was Church's name with angel wings surrounding it.

"What the fuck you 'bout to do, homie?" Native asked.

"I know, Fam, don't do it." Baby Dom continued.

"Baby Dom, shut the hell up," Mystro banged. "Get you some pussy first before you start trying to tell grown folks what to do."

"Baby Dom, here," Native said handing her some money. "Run cross the street and get me some

Utz Salt & Vinegar chips and a Pepsi. Grab something for yourself too.

Baby Dom reluctantly took the money and bopped toward the front door. "Stop her, Native," she yelled. "You gotta stop her. I don't like that girl, she sneaky." Baby Dom vanished out the door and into the street.

"Son, I know you gone over shawty, but I don't think you should ink her name on you," Native stated. "I mean that's permanent shit, Slim."

"Man, look, I know you may not be feeling Church, but that's my girl. We together now and soon she gonna be my wife." Mystro defended her love.

"Son, do you hear yourself," Native asked, "You sound crazy. That girl ain't serious 'bout you. I don't see her down here signed up to get inked with your name."

"Native, chill with your overprotective ass. Me and my boo good, relax." Mystro assured.

"Look, I ain't wanna blow shit up, but the other night at the Delta, Baby Dom said she saw Church handing some set of dick and balls some money. *Our money*, Mystro. Money that was from our tips," Native informed. "I don't think your girlfriend knows she's in a relationship, son."

Mystro was floored, she thought about what Native just laid out to her. She knew that Native never really liked Church, but she trusted her best friend, she wouldn't lie to her. At the same time, it was Baby Dom's ass that brought her the info and maybe she was confused on what she saw. Mystro loved Church and as her girlfriend, she wanted to give her the benefit of the doubt.

"Son, I'ma see what Church says 'bout that. If she did give a nigga some money, then she had a reason. But, it won't change my love for her. And right now, I wanna get my tat." Mystro told Native. "Let's do it, Blondie," she said to the tattoo artist, while lying back in the black leather reclining chair.

The white female artist rolled her chair passed a disappointed Native and up to Mystro's side. But as she dipped her needle into the black ink to get started, there was a loud boom, and within seconds they were submerged into complete darkness.

"What the fuck was that," Native jumped up and yelled.

"It ain't storming," Mystro said. "So why'd the power go out?"

# CHAPTER 14

Mystro and Church were sitting at the dining room table where they just finished their dinner. Church cooked Mystro's favorite meal of homemade beef meatloaf, mashed potatoes, cheese spinach and cornbread.

"Damn, baby, you told me you could cook but I thought you was bullshitting," Mystro said jokingly.

"Hmmm...I burn in the kitchen and in other places, as you already know," Church winked, grabbing Mystro's empty plate to put into the sink.

"Hey, sexy, I got something to show you." Mystro said walking up on Church in her small kitchen. "I want you to know I'm in, all the way in."

She unbuttoned her shirt and exposed her wife beater and brand new tattoo. Despite Baby Dom's wild ass attempt to prevent her from getting Church's name tatted on her by clipping the shop's power, Mystro went back alone a different day and completed the work.

"Mystro, wow...it's...uh...so big...wow," Church managed to say.

Mystro's chest deflated. What...you don't like it?" Mystro asked perplexed. "I thought you'd be sised."

"No, don't get me wrong, I'm flattered, but what made you do that?" Church inquired confused.

"What you mean? We together now. This just how I show you I'm trying to really be about you," Mystro explained.

"I think it's sweet, honey, I really do. It's just a little sudden. I mean we only been official for a few days. I wish you would've told me you was gonna do that first."

"Yeah, I know, but, I mean it ain't like we just met. We been sexing for a minute now," Mystro offered.

"Look, I like you, you know I do. But I think you need to slow up and not rush this thing between us."

"Slow up," Mystro asked. "Slow up how?"

"Baby, you coming at me full speed ahead—"

"So what you playing me," Mystro yelled, cutting Church off. "Like I'm some sucka ass dyke."

Church was startled. Except for the time in the gym parking lot, she had never seen Mystro snap like this. So she chose her words carefully before she replied.

"Mystro," she said grabbing her hands. "I'm not playing you, sweetie. I'm trying to keep it real with you. I told you, I am a person who needs financial stability. I mean look around, besides the fact that this house is too small for me, it's not even mine." Mystro looked around the cramped space. "I need to be cared for and taken care of, in all ways. Now I don't doubt you can care for me, but taking care of me financially is something totally different."

"But you saw us the other night, we killed it."

"Yes, but that's small change, baby, how far you think that will get us? I mean ya'll dance well and were very seductive, but that ain't big enough for me. I need serious income."

"Man, I don't know what you want me to do. I'm doing all I can. What do you want from me?" Mystro asked.

"Everything. I have to feel comfortable knowing you got me, in order for it to work, and right now I just don't. So until that time, let's not jump in this with both feet just yet, ok," Church asked, dropping Mystro's hands and sliding her arms around Mystro's waist looking up to her for an answer.

Mystro wasn't listening to what Church said. She knew that all she had to do was prove herself and that's what she planned on doing.

"Ok, baby, I'm with you. Can I ask you something," Mystro said bending down to steal a quick kiss. "The other night at the club Baby Dom said she saw you giving some money to a nigga, and it looked a little off. Did you?" She asked kissing on Church's neck.

"What," Church yelled pulling away and snatching her arms off Mystro. "That little trouble maker is lying. I caught her trying to pocket fifty dollars of ya'll's money. Did she tell you that shit," she paused. "Yeah, I bet you she didn't. Lying ass bitch."

"Come on, ma, Baby Dom has her shit wit' her, but she not gonna straight bank us." Mystro explained.

"Oh really, because I seem to recall how she did just that the night I met you."

Church had a point. Baby Dom had light fingers, but over the past couple weeks she had shown major change.

"I know people like her," Church continued. "She mad cuz she got caught and now she trying to turn the heat on me. I do not trust her, and you shouldn't either. But I guess it's going to boil down to who you really believe."

Mystro was torn. She needed answers and the truth.

# CHAPTER 15

Mystro had a lot on her mind and heart. She needed to go check on her father, and see about his wellbeing, it had been a while since she last saw him. Her father, Mack Mason, was being cared for in a hospice in Northern Virginia. Mystro hated hospitals and anything else that resembled them. Besides, every time she was in her pops company, he found a way to bring her down. So she dreaded their visits.

"What's up, Mack," Mystro said, coming into the room and greeting her father. She walked up to his bed, and planted a kiss on his baldhead, before pulling up a chair next to his bed to sit down. The room smelled of death. A scent most institutions like this favored, and Mystro felt nauseous.

Mack removed the oxygen mask from his face slowly to speak to his daughter. "Mystro," Mack said before coughing harshly, "I been waiting on you." His cough grew louder, and sounded as if it hurt his chest.

Although she did not have the best relationship with her daddy, she hated to watch him suffer.

"Mack, don't say too much. I just wanted to come check on you, but I don't want you to overdue it by trying to rap me out," Mystro laughed. It was her attempt to lighten the mood. "Take it easy."

Mack shook his head. "It's not gonna be," Mack paused before taking in more oxygen, "That easy too...keep me quiet. I know you don't fuck with me," He paused again. "But I'm the only father you got...and I ain't got much time left."

This is the shit she was talking about, she didn't come up there to be berated, but it was the same old stuff with Mack Mason every time. It was no wonder why she stayed gone.

"Come on, Mack, whatchu talking 'bout? You will be on your feet in no time." Mystro lied.

"Bullshit, you know the only way I leave...here...is bagged up." He pulled from his air supply.

Mack suffered from a rare form of cancer called Mesothelioma. He acquired the disease from working many years in construction, which exposed him to asbestos on a consistent basis, and things weren't getting any better.

"Aight, well that's not why I came through today," Mystro advised changing the subject. "I wanted to check and see how they treating you and let you know I'm doing fine. I got a job paying me decent wages and I'm in love with a beautiful woman. "She's the one, Mack, I'm telling you."

"Again," Mack sarcastically stated.

"What's that 'sposed to mean?" Mystro said angrily snatching her cap off her head.

"Mystro, you fall in love more times than they change my sheets around here," Mack said laughing before recovering his face with his mask.

Mystro was on fire. Her father had a way of pushing all of her buttons. She didn't understand why he couldn't just be happy for her.

"Mack, why do you do this," Mystro asked, placing her black Baltimore Ravens hat on her head backwards. "Do you want me to hate you, too?"

"What…you mean… like you hate your mother?"

Mystro had an alienated relationship with her father, but had no relationship with her mother, Melissa. She never knew her mother, and as she got older and older, she tried not to care.

"Mack, you know I don't like to talk about her," Mystro said.

"Look…you are going…to have…to face your issues about your…mother not being there…for you…sooner or later," Mack managed to say in between coughs and oxygen breaks.

Melissa White was a selfish type of bitch who only gave a fuck about two things, herself and singing in her band. She got pregnant by Mack after a one-night stand in Atlantic City. Mack was there gambling with his uncle when the most beautiful voice he ever heard took his attention from Blackjack. He smiled, waived, and waited for Melissa to finish her set to introduce himself. And before the sun rose over the Atlantic City beach, they were in his hotel suite fucking, raw. After their sex session, they went on with their lives and never spoke to each other again. In Mack's mind, it would be the last time he saw her.

By the time Melissa realized she was pregnant, she was already six months, and too far along for an abortion. She knew she had to have the baby, and never told a sole she was pregnant. Eight months in, while prepping in her hotel room to hit the road in a few days, she had an idea. She wanted to self induce her labor so that she could have her baby, and be ready to roll with the band when it was time. She did strenuous exercises, and took two tablespoons of caster oil. Her home remedies worked, and by the next morning, Melissa's water broke. Her only child was ready to be born.

"Mack, the only issues I have is the fact that for what seemed like everyday of my life, you made it known that you had to give up everything to become a father to me," Mystro yelled while leaping from her chair. "I ain't ask to be born you know."

"What kind...of...man would I have been...if I abandoned you too?"

Mystro walked over to the window and stared out, temporarily ignoring her father. She hated confronting her past, it was too much to handle. She had to grow up watching kids around her interact with their mothers, knowing that eight hours after giving birth to her, Melissa abandoned her in the hospital just to make her singing gig on time.

The only motherly act Melissa ever did was naming her daughter. And that was only because Melissa grew tired of the nurse barging into her hospital room with the birth certificate papers, disturbing her from making up her face. So on the last time, Melissa looked up at her TV and noticed a (Maestro) conducting an orchestra, and to shut the simple nurse bitch down, she told her to name the baby *Mystro Mason*. She flipped the spelling of her first name up and gave her Mack's last name.

"Mack, I know you stepped up and I appreciate it, but you fucked Melissa, not me. You could have left me in the hospital too," Mystro blurted out over her shoulder from the window.

"You don't think I wanted too," Mack asked. "I was twenty-two years old with no responsibilities and not a care in the world when they called me about you." He continued with a newfound burst of breath and stamina. "Had Melissa not put my name on that birth certificate as the father, they would not have ever known who I was. But instead of running…I saw it as a sign. I needed to slow down and take care of my responsibilities as a man…so I did."

"Right," Mystro said turning completely around to face her father. "You decided to step up but it seems like in return for it, you tried to make me feel like I owed you. That shit ain't fair, Mack."

"Look...I...wasn't the best...father in the world, but I wasn't the worst either. I thought I did a decent job...of raising...you...to be...respectful and honest. I tried...not to bring a lot...of chicks...around you...because I saw how...you got too...attached to 'em." Mack sucked in more air before continuing. "And yeah, maybe I shouldn't have been...so hard on you... or blamed you, but I ain't know...no better." Mack paused to look into Mystro's eyes.

Mystro wiped the single tear that streamed down her face and looked down at her father.

"I'm dying...and I don't have...much time," Mack stressed again, pausing for more oxygen. "I...need...you...to hear me, Mystro," he coughed. "I'm...proud of you...and I love you, but you...need to...stop forcing these relationships...on these...random...chicks you meet out there. They are not your mother...and never will be. I'm afraid...that one day...and soon...you gonna snap...if it don't play out...in your favor. What will you do...then," Mack finished. "The judge won't be so lenient with you this time." Mystro thought about what her pop said. She knew he was right. He was the only family she had, he did teach her respect and cared for her the best way he knew how. But she just didn't get why he couldn't understand that this situation with Church was different and not like the several other relationships she had in the past. She knew there was only one way to convince him. She had to prove it.

"Look, Mack, my new shawty is different. She's career oriented, she's fly and she loves me," Mystro said, excitedly standing next to her father's bedside. "I'ma bring her up here next time I come, and you'll see for yourself when you meet her. You gonna change your mind."

Mack removed the oxygen mask from his face and stared at his daughter. He looked at her hazel eyes that mirrored his own eye color and smiled. *She turned out to be everything I would want in a son or daughter. I pray that she gets some help before she ruins her life or someone else's.* Mack thought.

"Ok, Mystro...you win. Come here," Mack said, holding his weak arms open to embrace her into his frail body.

Mystro leaned down to hug her father. He pulled her in, with all the strength he could muster, for a long embrace. Mystro was so close now, she could smell the foul odor coming from his breath, but placed it out of her mind. She didn't want to ruin the moment.

"I...love you...Mystro," Mack said to his daughter barely above a whisper, trying to fight back his emotions.

"I love you too, daddy," Mystro said choking back her tears. It was the first time since she was a little girl that she called him daddy instead of Mack.

"Get some rest, I'll see you again soon." Mystro kissed her father for the last time before leaving his room. And before she could leave out of the hospice completely, Mack Mason flat lined.

# CHAPTER 16

Mystro was alone at *Bar 100*, which was a mixed culture lesbian lounge in the uptown section of Washington DC. She laid her pops to rest two days ago. It was one of the hardest things she ever had to do in her life so far. Seeing the man who took care of her, who she loved despite their differences, lying there life-less broke her down.

She reflected back on the last two times she kissed her daddy. The night in the hospice, minutes before he died, and the day of the funeral, right before they closed his casket. She thought about the difference in how in one kiss his body was warm and still held life. And in the other kiss, his body felt like ice. Mystro was a wreck, and she didn't know what direction to take with her life. Although Native and even Baby Dom were both right there by her side for the entire ordeal, Church wasn't.

Mystro could not understand why Church could be so cold. She did not come to the funeral nor did she call to check up on her. Mystro was hurt by her inaction, how could the woman she wanted to be her wife, not be there for her when she needed her the most? She needed answers now. She was angry, hurt and worst of all she was drunk.

"Shawty," Mystro yelled attempting to get her bartender's attention.

"Another one, sweetie," the white bar temptress asked. She had been trying to flirt all night, but Mystro had a one-track mind and didn't pick up on her advances.

"Naw, naw…I'm good, ma," Mystro advised, slightly slurring her words. "Can you give me my check, I gotta press," she requested, reaching into the back pocket of her black Levis for her wallet.

The bartender gave Mystro her tab and without even looking at it, Mystro gave her a fifty-dollar bill and stood up to make her exit. Once she was on her feet, she felt the results of five peach Ciroc shots and three Budweiser's. As she got herself together, she noticed the bartender staring at her.

"What's up, shawty," Mystro asked. "I ain't give you enough?"

"No, it was more than enough, matter fact, here's your change," she said handing Mystro ten dollars back.

Mystro took the money from her and left a five-dollar bill for the tip.

"Are you gonna be ok," the bartender asked.

"I'm straight, shawty, I'm on a mission," Mystro said before heading out the lounge.

* * * **CHURCH'S HOUSE**\*\*\*

Mystro pulled up and parked across the small street from Church's house. She noticed Church's BMW sitting in the driveway and immediately drew heat.

*'She got the nerve to be home and not calling me.'* Mystro thought. She had enough.

"Fuck this shit," Mystro said snatching open her car door to make her entrance onto the damp road. Once outside, she slammed the door and trotted across the street heading to the door "Church," Mystro yelled banging on her front door. "Chuuuuuurrrcch...open this door," she shouted.

After only a minute, Church snatched open her door and stepped out on to the porch. "Mystro, what the hell is wrong with you," she banged.

"Fuck you mean what is wrong with me? Where you been? Why you ain't been taking my calls?" Mystro roll called several questions to her.

"Keep your voice down, do you know what time it is," Church asked.

"I don't give a fuck 'bout what time it is. Where you been?" Mystro barked snatching Church's elbow and pulling her close to her.

Church immediately recognized the scent of alcohol on her breath. "Baby, calm down," she said putting her petite hand on Mystro's chest. "You been drinking and you are in no condition to discuss this tonight. How about you go get some sleep and we can talk tomorrow," Church suggested.

"It is tomorrow," she yelled, referring to the fact that it was after midnight. "Look at this," Mystro stated releasing her grip on Church and snatching up her black Hugo Boss T-shirt exposing her tattoo of Church's name. "Do this shit mean anything to you?" She asked.

Church remained silent.

"My daddy died," Mystro broke down. "My daddy died and you don't give a fuck," she continued with streams of tears fleeing her eyes without permission.

"Baby," Church said walking up on Mystro and caressing her face. "I'm so sorry, I didn't know, is there anything I can do?"

Mystro used the inside of her shirt collar to wipe her tears in one motion. "Yeah, can I stay here tonight, I just need to be under you."

"Uhhh, ummm, no, baby, tonight is not good," Church said.

"What…Why not?"

"Because I'm just getting back in town. I've only been here for an hour and I'm completely exhausted. Just go home and get some rest and I'll call you tomorrow," Church instructed.

"That's how you carrying it," Mystro asked. "I tell you my daddy died and I wanna be with you and you tell me you exhausted?" Church stood voiceless and motionless. "You know what, fuck you, Church." Mystro yelled as she stumbled back to walk to her car.

Church watched Mystro get in her Maxima and pull off in haste. But before she could get back inside, she heard a loud crash not too far from her house, coming from the same direction Mystro drove away.

# CHAPTER 17
## ONE MONTH LATER

Mystro and Native were at Bowie Town Center walking around window-shopping. Ever since Mack died, they had taken a little bit of a break from performing so Mystro could grieve. Not to mention the fact that her and Church had not spoken since the night she confronted her at her house.

Secretly, Mystro was at a loss. There were days where she posted up, down the block from Church's house to keep tabs on her, although, it never amounted to much. She would see Church coming and going, but always alone. Then she had an epiphany, and her father's dying words resonated with her. She didn't want to have to stalk women and force love upon them. Mystro decided to try and give her some space, and it was hard. She missed talking to her, holding her, and especially making love to her.

Now, their pockets were hurting, and rent was once again due, so the grieving and heartache would have to wait. It was time to pick up the broken pieces of her life and make money.

"Slim, did you call up the Delta to hold our spot for Friday," Native asked Mystro.

"Oh, naw, let me go head and call now though." Mystro reached into her black Nike basketball shorts pocket to retrieve her iPhone.

"Hello, do ya'll still have slots open to perform on Friday?"

"Yep, what's your name," The club manager asked.

"This Mystro, and me and my homie dance under the name Hersband Material."

"Oh…yeah, umm, my bad, Mystro, we booked up."

"Whatchu mean you booked up? You just said you had an opening." Mystro looked over at Native.

"I'm sorry I forgot we had just filled up right before you called. Try us next week." The manager hung up the phone, before she could dispute.

Mystro looked confused as she pulled the phone off her ear to see if he really did hang up.

He did.

"Son, this mothafucka on some bullshit. You heard my first question right," Mystro asked Native for reassurance.

"Yeah, you asked him if they still had slots." Native cosigned.

"Right, the bamma told me yeah and asked for my name. Soon as I told him, he switched up. Talking 'bout, *naw they booked*," she explained still holding up the phone near her face.

"You don't think they trying to carry us on purpose do you," Native asked.

"I'm not sure, but I know if we don't perform we gonna be short on rent again."

"Shit," Native shouted. "Mommy gonna be coming for our heads too. How much you got now?"

Mystro dug into her pocket and retrieved her wallet. She quickly counted all the bills. "Son, I got forty on me and about thirty in my account."

"Thirty in your account? I thought you was stashing more than that," Native said.

"I was, but you know I had to put it to Mack's funeral," Mystro advised sadly.

"Damn…right. My bad, slim."

"How much you got?" Mystro asked changing the subject back.

"Shit I ain't got but thirty myself," Native advised. "And if we ain't got at least the whole two bills for mommy, she liable to go ham. Fuck. This is the last thing we need."

## \* \* BACK AT HOME\* \*

When Mystro pulled up on their block, she felt something was up. Her thoughts were confirmed when she saw Baby Dom running off the porch frantically, in their direction, with her arms filled with clothes.

"Baby Dom, fuck you doing?" Mystro yelled out of her open car window.

"Fam, mommy up there going. She tossing ya'll shit out," Baby Dom yelled.

"What," Native yelled throwing the car door open and jumping out.

"BD, move out the way so I can park," Mystro instructed.

She needed to make sure Baby Dom was out of the street completely. She could not rely on her passenger side mirror to use as a guide to not hit anything on that side anymore. The night she left Church's house drunk and pissed, she accidently jumped the curb and hit a dumpster, knocking her mirror smooth off. That was the loud crash noise Church heard.

Baby Dom immediately moved out of the way and followed behind Native who was already heading to the house.

"Mommy, what you doing," Native asked, picking up her clothes and shoes that were now decorating the front porch. She was heated too, she cherished her gear and her mother was totally disrespecting that fact.

"Do you have my rent?" Margaret stopped her eviction tactics to ask.

"Mommy, come on man, you ain't have to do us like this. You know we gonna pay you," Native pled. "You act like we strangers or something."

Mystro trotted up to the porch after parking and could not believe the sight before her. It looked like a Downtown Locker Room store exploded. Most of their belongings draped the porch.

"*Gonna pay* me," Margaret repeated. "I don't wanna hear that shit. You know you late, and I told you what would happen if my money wasn't on time. Now do you have it or not?"

"Ms. Houston, we only have half of it now," Mystro chimed in. "We would have had it all, but I had to use my savings for my daddy's funeral expenses."

"Yeah, man, that's what I was trying to tell you —"

"Shut up, Native," Margaret scolded.

Baby Dom laughed out loud before catching herself and continuing to help pick up their stuff.

"Mystro, I am sympathetic to your situation. You know I am, but the white man don't wanna hear no excuses when he come asking me for the mortgage. I got to pay him or we all outta here, and on the street," Margaret explained. "Now, I'ma give ya'll one more week to get the rest of my money. But if you do not have it by then, you both got to go," she firmly stated. "I'm not taking care of no grown ass women."

"Yes, ma'am." Mystro replied.

Margaret held her hand out for the half payment. Mystro dug into her pocket and retrieved the money she had. Native did the same, and they handed it to Margaret who took it and walked back towards the door to go inside.

"Damn, mommy, you cold," Native said angrily. "Can you at least help take some of this stuff back inside?"

Mystro and Baby Dom both burst into laughter.

Native didn't crack a smile. "I'm serious, shit she the one got all this stuff out here man." Native fumed, while she wiped off her construction Timbs and placed them back into their box.

"Native, you lucky I didn't sell half that shit on Greg's List, and get my damn rent money." Margaret stood in the doorway. "Now, I mean it. Have my hundred dollars by next Friday or you out on your asses." Margaret walked inside, slamming the screen door behind her.

"We in trouble," Mystro confessed. "She not fucking around with us no more. We need cash now."

# CHAPTER 18

"Slim, hand me the gun oil and the rod," Mystro asked.

She and Native were sitting at home in the living room doing nothing. Mystro decided to clean the resident .32 caliber gun. They had been in the house for most of the week following the Porch Massacres and were bored stupid.

"Man, I can't take this shit, son," Native shouted out. "I'm losing my mind. I ain't been out this house, I ain't got no pussy, I ain't got no new gear. I'm suffering, son."

"You be aight, champ. It ain't even been a week," Mystro said laughing. "Why you don't call Ife? I'm sure she would love to slide through and tighten you up in more ways than one," Mystro suggested.

"Man, I ain't fucking wit' that broad no more, she crazy as cat shit." Native flipped through the channels on the DVR.

"You gonna fuck around and marry that chick, watch," Mystro joked. "Remember I said that shit too."

"Never," Native yelled. "I'll fuck a nigga before I get married to anybody, let alone Ife's ass. Bet that," Native confessed.

"Yeah, ok." Mystro continued to laugh and clean the gun.

There was a rhythmic knock on the door indicating it could only be one person, Baby Dom. Native got up to answer it, while Mystro packed up all her weapon cleaning paraphernalia.

"What's up, killa," Native said to Baby Dom as she opened the door wide to let her inside. They decided to give her another chance and let her in the house, after she didn't snatch their belongings off the porch for profit.

"Ain't shit, fam. Where ya'll been," Baby Dom asked coming into the living room, and eyeing Mystro while she stash the gun and cleaning kit under the couch.

"We been right here, day in and day out. Not doing shit," Native yelled flopping on the couch, after closing and locking the door.

"Native got cabin fever, BD," Mystro said laughing, removing her latex gloves.

"You sick, Fam," Baby Dom approached Native, attempting to feel her head for a fever.

"Fuck no, nigga, get off me." Native pushed her hand away.

"Naw, cabin fever is a figure of speech. It means somebody tired of being cooped up in they crib," Mystro explained.

"Ohhhh…aight. But why you cooped up?"

"We broke, nigga. Ain't got no ends to do nothing," Native answered.

"Oh is that all, shit as long as I got it, ya'll do too," Baby Dom said, digging into her grey Nike sweatpants pocket to retrieve her money.

Mystro and Native looked at each other in shock. Baby Dom never ceased to amaze them.

## * * HOURS LATER* *

With the money Baby Dom provided, she treated them to Pizza and alcohol. They made a liquor store run first, and purchased Ciroc and beer. Once they were back home, they ordered pepperoni pizza from the delivery spot that made everything fresh. They kicked it old school in the house, and had more fun than they have had in weeks. It was just what they needed after a week of nothingness.

"Son, I'm 'bout to hit the Delta up and make sure we good for Friday," Native advised reaching for her phone to make the call. "Because all this shit is cool, but it ain't making us no money." The phone rung a few times before someone answered. "Yeah, what's up, I'm calling to get a spot on the lineup for *this* Friday. It's not too late is it?"

"Ummm, naw—" The man on the phone stopped short. "Wait…what's your name?"

"Native, from the duo Hersband Material," she stated.

"Ok, well, we booked up still. But if something opens up, we'll call you." He hung up the phone.

"Man, that's some bullshit," Native yelled slamming her phone onto the couch. "Something ain't right, son. Every time we call they got slots, until we mention the name Hersband Material."

"Maybe ya'll should change your name then," Baby Dom suggested, biting into a slice.

"That ain't what I'm talking about," Native shouted. "The shit is starting to seem personal."

"What you thinking," Mystro asked. "You think we being blackballed?"

"I'm feeling like we are. I mean two weeks straight...that raggedy ass club popping like that? Naw, the word has been put out on us, slim. We been cut off, and you know by who." Native deduced.

"Should I call her," Mystro asked disappointed and nervous about having to hear Church's voice.

"Yeah, I mean I don't fuck with her like that, but if anybody would know what's up it's her."

Baby Dom rolled her eyes and sipped her beer.

Mystro unplugged her cell phone from the charger, and scrolled through her calls looking for Church's number. When she located it she took a deep breath, before hitting the call button. After three rings, Church picked up.

"Hey stranger," Church greeted.

Mystro's stomach fluttered when she heard her voice. "What's up, Church," Mystro said dryly, trying to conceal her excitement.

"So I'm guessing you found out you can't get no love at the spot without me, huh?" Church asked.

Mystro's mouth dropped open. "So you been telling them bamma's to keep us off the books on purpose? Why would you even come off like that?"

Native jumped up, and attempted to put her ear near the phone to hear her answer. Mystro didn't like their faces touching so she pushed her back.

"Mystro, I understand that you were upset about me not being there for you and all, but you had no right cutting me off like that," Church said. "If it wasn't for me, ya'll wouldn't even be getting it like that. I made Hersband Material not you.

"Cutting you off, shawty I don't recall you putting no calls in to me either," Mystro walked out of the living room in search of privacy. "And now you messing with my paper? What the fuck you want with me?"

"I told you, I want everything. And, I have called you, you just chose not to take my calls," Church lied. She wanted them to come back begging, which is exactly what they did. "I mean why wouldn't I want to hear from you? As a matter of fact, I called yesterday twice, and the phone kept going to voicemail."

"Damn, my phone prolly acting up again. It gets to tripping sometimes," Mystro confessed.

Church was elated she got away with her lie. "You see what I'm saying, you coming all hard at me when you in the wrong. Sometimes I think you believe I'm out to hurt you. Like I don't care about you."

"That ain't it. It's just been a heavy period for me," she paused. When Native peeked in the room Mystro remembered the purpose of the call. "So can you get us back on the list, we really need to make some money."

"I'm sure you do, but since ya'll tried it with me, I started managing another act," Church explained. "My time is valuable, and I wanted you to realize it. I didn't wanna do it like this though."

Mystro's eyes widened. "So you saying we out? We need that money, Church."

"Well, I can see what I can do, but I can't promise you much," Church stated. "Even if I get you back on, the money won't be the same. You are sharing the spotlight now. My new duo is raking in the long dough, and the ladies are screaming their names."

"Look, Church, it was bad communication on both our parts, but it won't happen again. Hook us up, baby," Mystro begged. "Trust me, we'll make it worth your while."

"Ok, I'll get ya'll on for Friday, although, I really feel ya'll may be done as performers though," Church rubbed in. "But keep an open mind, cuz if the dancing is in fact done, I got another idea on how ya'll can make bigger paper. I just hope you'll be down."

# CHAPTER 19

Mystro and Native were just arriving at the Delta nightclub to perform, since Church had them put back into the rotation. The mood was sullen as the two friends moved around the small dressing room in silence. They prepared to put their outfits on to do their routine, until they heard loud screaming coming from upstairs.

"What the fuck are they hollering for," Mystro asked, while she whipped her head around to face Native.

"Nigga, I'm down here with you," She said. "How the fuck should I know what's popping upstairs," Native replied sarcastically.

"Shit, ain't but one way to find out." Mystro put her shorts back on to head up to investigate.

"Hold up, cuz. I'm going too," Native advised getting up from her chair.

The moment they stepped out the dressing room, they saw only a few women scattered around the lower level of the dance club, which was odd because it was normally packed. If everybody was upstairs, something special must be happening and they wanted to know what.

"Where the fuck everybody go," Native asked.

"Come on, son," Mystro instructed as they jotted up the steps, two by two, quickly reaching the top.

When they looked towards the floor, they could not believe the sight before them. Two younger looking Dom's were on the stage performing and the crowd was eating them up. One of the Doms had long silky hair flowing down her back and her red button down shirt was open, revealing her black sports bra. The other wore a short gold curly bush, and she kept lowering her black Gucci shades as if she was looking for a special lady.

"Who the fuck is them *Mindless Behavior* looking dykes," Mystro asked.

"What the fuck," Native replied, scanning the crowd. There wasn't a woman around without at least a dollar bill in her hand. "And these bitches is loving 'em, too. Them baby dykes look like they twelve years old."

They may have looked twelve but they were making adult money. The young Dom act was turning the club out, and they were doing well too. They were kissing women in the mouth, gyrating and hopping all over the floor like rabbits. The youngin's were about their money and it was official when Mystro's eyes landed at Silky Hair's next tactic. Mystro almost lost her skittles when she saw her biting on Big Greasy's nipple through her blouse.

"I don't think they care about how old they are, champ. Look at all the money they banking," Mystro replied in awe.

"Yeah, and look who collecting that bank too," Native stated angrily.

That's when they both focused on who was collecting their tips, Church. She was smiling widely like a proud mother, as she scooped up the money falling from the sky.

"Fuck this, come on, man. Let's go get ready," Native instructed.

*  *  **A HOUR LATER**  *  *

Hersband Material had taken the stage in the same outfits, using the same music and routine and as a result, they only made enough money to pay their back rent and buy a few drinks. After their tired performance, they were in the back of the club sipping on their drinks completely blown, trying to figure out where they went wrong.

"What did I tell you," Church yelled over the music approaching their table. "Things have changed and so must we."

"What you talking about," Native shouted with an attitude. She hated her in more ways than one.

"I told you, Mystro," Church started in her attempt to ignore the pissy mode Native displayed.

"The performing ain't the same here anymore. Women want something different. They want a variety, and your show although good, is not cutting it. The money you earned tonight was evidence of that. It was mediocre."

"You seemed to do alright," Native responded, remembering all of the bills she collected from the Mindless Behavior looking Doms. Plus the percentage she earned from their performance, although small.

"Well that's me, I'm talking about you," she said closing her eyes.

"So that's your group too," Mystro said.

"Yep, because ain't nobody have time to wait around and see if you would get over your attitude with me or not. I went out and got two young, fresh Dom's to get that money. They don't give me no back talk and they prove to me that they are professionals," Church looked at Native, "Which is more than I can say for some people."

"That's some cold ass shit, shawty," Native said to Church. "One disagreement, and she cuts us off like an extra long toenail. And you fucked around and got this bitch's name tatted on you." Native shook her head. "That could never be me."

Mystro looked at Native shocked. "Native, what I do with my body is my business, champ, you know that."

"Yeah, but you my son and this chick don't respect you, or me."

"What do you mean, Native," Church inquired. "You have to earn respect before it's given."

"Native didn't mean anything by it, baby. She just a little heated cuz we ain't make what we thought we would." Mystro was trying to avoid a bad outcome.

"Slim, I know this your shawty and shit, but we talking business now. No disrespect, man. You know you my fam, but I gotta say what I'm feeling," Native rambled.

Mystro shook her head and grabbed her beer to take a sip indicating she's out of it.

"Church, you got us all pumped up, and kept pulling Mystro to get me back in the routine just to up and leave us high and dry? I mean you act like we was trying to cut you off--"

"Oh ya'll weren't?" Church interrupted. "I don't hear from ya'll in weeks and then I hear that ya'll been calling up here trying to get put on without me. What's that sound like to you?" Church argued back. "Sounds to me like you trying to cut me out of my fee."

"Whatever, moe. It's fucked up and you know it." Native grabbed her beer and sat back in her seat disconnecting from the argument.

"Look, baby, me and you had some issues and as a result, it carried over into the three of us and our business. It was wrong but how do we move past it," Mystro asked, trying to bring the focus back to what was next.

"Well, I have an idea, but it will involve both of you once again." Church said cutting her eyes to Native. "Are you with it or not?"

"I'm here ain't I," Native shot, seeing how Church looked at her.

Church laughed and shook her head. "Ok, my plan is to have you two fulfill women's fantasies."

"What does that mean," Mystro asked. "Was that not what we were doing?"

"No, I mean you were doing all you could do in this club, but I'm talking about doing more, and making more."

"Shawty, not for nothing, but some of us got places to go. Spit it out," Native yelled, impatiently.

Church rolled her eyes. "Look around this club. What do you see?"

"Women," both Mystro and Native replied simultaneously, as they often did.

"Duh, but what are they doing," Church asked searching for more detail.

Both Mystro and Native briefly scanned the room and observed the women of the club. They noticed how some of them were dancing, some were drinking and some talking. But, they also zeroed in on several women who were staring them down.

"You talking about how Biggie Dom and them keep staring at us," Mystro asked.

"Yes, the women who are staring at you are some of your biggest fans," Church stated. "And they can be some of your biggest sponsors too, if you let them."

"Can you get to the point," Native said sarcastically.

"Because they are your biggest fans, they will pay big money for you to be with them," Church finally said. "But you have to go all the way."

There was an awkward pause until Mystro finally understood what Church was getting at. "Baby, are you talking about fucking for money," she asked.

Native stared Church down with a surprised look, while waiting for an answer too.

"Yes, and it will make what tips you used to earn here look like lunch money," Church said with a confident smirk. "I can do that for you, unless you got a better idea, like staying here and trying to compete with my other group."

# CHAPTER 20

"Church," Native said into the phone. "I'm not too sure 'bout this here."

Native was sitting in her mother's 2006 Honda Accord talking on her cell with Church, who she just called when she arrived in front of the house she was instructed to go to.

"Native, don't get scared now, that girl is waiting on you. You have to go up to the door to get her. Then, ya'll have dinner reservations at *Marvin's* uptown. Now be a big Dom and go get your lady. And remember, this one is paying for the perfect date, so mind your manners and be a gentleman. Now you can do that right?"

"Don't play me, shawty."

"I'm serious." Church replied.

"And so am I," Native stated. "And while I got you on the phone, I hope you don't try and play my homie. This move you got us on makes it seem like you our pimp instead of her woman."

"I keep telling you that me and Mystro's business is our own."

"And it still will be that whether you take my advise or not. Mystro can't be hurt again, I need you to know that. I care about her more than I care about this money shit."

"I won't hurt her, you don't have to worry about it," Church explained. "Now get in there and get your date. Your public awaits."

"Yeah aight," Native reluctantly said before ending the call.

Mystro and Native were hesitant on the plans that Church had for them, but after some careful thought and the whistling sounds their empty pockets made, they gave in. Mystro didn't like the idea, but after Church reassured her this was the best option for their long-term relationship, she slowly got on board.

Native arrived at the door of her date and knocked. She took a deep breath before the door sprang open. If she could, she would have turned around and broke out of there quickly, after seeing what the girl looked like. She had to be at least six feet tall, if not taller, and awkwardly shaped. She wore coke bottle thick glasses that she kept pushing up on her nose, and she was *Olive Oil* type bony.

"Hi, I'm Native, your date for the evening. These are for you." Native handed the girl a bouquet of flowers. "Are you ready to go, beautiful?" Native almost gagged from that lie.

Olive Oil blushed and took the flowers out of her hand. "Yes, I've been waiting on you all day," she replied, before taking in a big whiff of her gift.

"Then let's do it." Native said offering her elbow for her to grab.

## * * * **MARVIN'S** ***

"So tell me a little more about yourself, Yolanda. You from DC," Native asked while cutting her steak.

"Yes, I was born and raised here and I know I'll die here too. DC is my world. I never even been outside of it, and don't want to."

*'What the hell? She know she'll die here too? Moe is a retard. Please kill yourself. I'm so fucking ready to go. Bitch, eat quicker. I hope she really just wants a date and not a fuck. I have no idea how I would go about climbing this tree.'* Native's mind rambled while she smiled in *Olive Oil's* face pretending she was really listening.

Yolanda ran her mouth the entire time and Native could not take much more. "…So that's what I plan to do in five years. Anyway, this food was so good, Native. Don't you think," Yolanda asked.

"Yes, this is one of my favorite spots. I'm glad you like it too. Do you want any dessert? Their *Warm Toffee Cake* is like that," Native advised, secretly hoping she said no.

"No, I couldn't eat another bite. Are you ready to go?"

*'Hell yeah I'm ready, bitch. Let's bounce!'* Native thought. "I'm ready if you are." she said.

## * * * BACK AT OLIVE OIL'S ***

"I see you have a fireplace, do you want me to light a fire so we can have our nightcaps in front of it?" Native asked, trying to continue in the gentleman, romance fashion she was being paid for.

"No," she replied with a crazed look in her eyes. "I just want you to sit over there, so that I can look at you."

Native picked up on the look and was frightened. *'I hope I don't have to two piece this big bitch.'* Native thought.

All of the sudden, Yolanda charged Native who was sitting on her brown leather couch. She ran full speed at her, hopped on her lap with her extra long legs draping over Native's thighs and threw her wet sloppy mouth onto Native's. She slobbed her down, and Native immediately began to feel nauseous.

Native tried her best to keep the rhythm of the kiss, except there was no rhythm, and every move seemed to be all over the place. She needed to take control, so she could wrap this situation up soon.

Native shifted her body to have Yolanda sitting on the couch now, while she was over top of her. Native figured that if she rushed her like that, she either liked it fast and rough, or she had no clue how to have sex any other way. This was a good thing for

Native, she was gonna bang this bitch's ass out real quickly and get the fuck!

Native lifted up Olive Oil's dress, and ripped off her big draws. She exposed her huge pussy with a landing strip designed in her pubic hair. *'She had the nerve to try and pretty this long ass box up,'* Native thought.

"How you want it baby," Native asked.

"I want you to lick my pussy dry," Olive Oil requested.

*'Lick you dry, that ain't even possible, dummy,'* Native thought. She needed to make this chick cum quick. She already felt her dinner rising in her throat, and wasn't sure about how much longer she could hang around.

Native reminded herself about her future payout, and went to work. She parted Yolanda's pussy lips with her unwashed fingers to expose her pink clit. Surprisingly, even though everything else on her body was long, her clit was concealed within the softness of her lips. Native used more fingers on both her hands to completely pull her pussy open, and covered her clit with her warm mouth. Before Native could even bare down onto her sex button, Yolanda screamed out in ecstasy.

That quickly, she busted a nut, and Native was confused. "You came, Yolanda?"

"Oh, my...God, yes," Yolanda yelled. "You were great, and the best I ever had."

Native was completely thrown off, but immediately jumped up, since her work was done.

Yolanda pulled her dress down and sat up straight on her couch. She reached over on the coffee table, and handed Native a paper towel for her to wipe her juices off of her fingers and chin.

"So, would you like to watch a movie with me while you finish your drink," she asked. "I'm not in a rush, so I can stay with you longer if you can stay with me.

"Oh no, I can't. I had a great time, but I gotta break out. Have a good night." Native made a beeline for the door.

As soon as she was outside she threw up right on Yolanda's sidewalk. After spilling her guts, literally, she pulled out her cell phone to call Church.

Now back in her mother's borrowed car, Church answered the phone after the second ring.

"Shawty, don't ever send me on no wild ass freak show call like that again—"

"Native," Church yelled cutting her off. "You will go wherever the hell I tell you to go, or continue to be the same broke-busted-dyke you were before. I've taken your shit for long enough. It's time you realize that the only one who's running Hersband Material is me."

# CHAPTER 21

"This is completely insane, Church," Mystro yells out while buttoning up her red shirt. "How can you be cool wit' sending me out to kick it and fuck another broad?" Mystro grabbed her eight-inch brown rubber dildo and black leather harness out of her duffle bag.

"It's simple, sweetie, this is how we make our living now. Some people go to a nine to five job and get paid. Others are a bit more creative and work less for more. That's what we do.

Mystro was at Church's house getting dressed to go out on her arranged date. Although she was prepping to leave, she was completely against it.

"Yeah, but how can you not care about another woman getting what you got? I mean dancing is one thing, I can see that. But fucking? Come on, shawty. It would be no way in the world I could send you out to do no shit like that if I was you –"

"But you not me," Church interrupted. "So don't concern yourself with it. I'm worrying about our family...the family you said you wanted with me." She was angry. Mystro stopped fixing her black tie and shot Church an evil look.

Church noticed the glance Mystro gave and realized she might have gone too far with her word play. She needed to regain her composure before she started an argument and caused Mystro to stand her date up, resulting in losing money.

"Listen, baby," Church said facing her, and grabbing her tie to help her finish dressing. "You have to trust me. We stand to make good money. This move is for our security and future together. That is, if you want a future with me." She looked up into Mystro's eyes while sliding up the knot she finished on her tie.

Mystro stared back into Church's eyes and took a deep breath before speaking. "If this is for our future together, then I'll do it, but only if you move in with me."

Her eyes widened. "Move in with you," Church repeated. "Where, at Native's mother's house," she laughed.

"Fuck no," she yelled, "its barely enough room there for us now. Naw, I'm talking about getting an apartment and having you move in with me." Mystro waited for her answer.

"Uh, Mystro," Church started while she turned away and looked for Mystro's shoes. "Why would I move out of a house and into an apartment? I mean what about the dance studio I built in the basement? I'm already set up here."

"Shawty, I'm not 'bout to go out this joint and sex a chick for our future, just to have you continue to lay up in this house. This shit ain't even yours, or did you forget it belongs to a set of dick and balls that be lunching 'bout you giving him rent and shit?" Mystro yelled with intensity. "It's time to start our life together."

"Baby, come on," Church said as she walked over to the bedroom window to look outside. "Look the town car just pulled up. You gotta go, can't we talk about this later," she asked in her attempt to dismiss the question again.

Mystro took a seat on the brown leather bench that sat at the foot of the king sized bed. "Shawty, I'm not leaving out that door until you tell me what I need to hear," she said while leaning back onto the mattress. "Are we gonna do this thing or not?"

*'Who the fuck does she think she's talking to, I make the damn rules not her,'* Church thought. She looked at Mystro from the window and decided to play her game. Besides, she had to get her on the way to her date, because the girl had already paid in advance and Church did not believe in refunds. "Ok, you win," she replied walking up to Mystro. "I will move in with you once you get a condo," she changed it up.

"You will," Mystro asked excitedly jumping up from the bench. "Wait, condo, I said an apartment, Church."

"And I said a condo. I know you don't think you gonna keep a bitch of my caliber in a run down apartment, do you? No, darling, I want a view of the water, so you need to get to work. And it starts with going on this date."

* * * **PRESIDENTIAL SUITES** * * *

Mystro arrived at the hotel suite door and knocked firmly. *'Damn, I should've taken one more vodka shot in the car,'* she thought while she waited. She needed courage for what she was about to do.

The door to the suite parted and Mystro took in the beautiful woman who opened it. She was nowhere near how Mystro pictured she would look. Especially after hearing the horror story Native told her from her first date.

"Damn," Mystro said still standing in the hallway of the hotel. "Oh, my bad, I mean, hi, I'm Mystro, your date for the evening." She was in awe of the woman's sex appeal. The woman was slightly older than Mystro at thirty-five, but she was physically on point. She wore a red silk negligee with black lace sides and a matching silk robe. Her Channel No. 5 perfume leaped off her body and teased Mystro's nose. She was thick, with an ass that could be seen from the front.

"Hi, Mystro, I'm Denver, pleased to meet you." Denver reached out to shake Mystro's hand. "Please come in," Mystro walked inside the suite and handed her the bouquet of roses she had for her.

"These are for you," she said giving her the flowers and watched as she took them into the bathroom to put them in water. *'Shit, her ass is even phatter from the back, mercy,'* Mystro thought.

"The roses are nice, thank you. Can I offer you a drink before you get started," Denver asked while walking over to the suite's blue marble bar.

"Yes, thanks, you have any vodka." Mystro walked into the living room portion of the plush suite.

"I have *Kettle One,* is that ok?" Denver held the bottle of vodka up for Mystro to see from across the room.

"Yes, that's cool," Mystro walked toward the bar to retrieve her drink. Denver poured the liquor in the glass over ice cubes and handed it to Mystro. She took the glass and shot the liquor down quickly. She noticed the iPod doc on the bar. "Ok, Denver, go over to the couch and have a seat," she instructed feeling her confidence kick in from all the alcohol she consumed. While Denver followed her orders, Mystro plugged her iPod into the doc and selected her *Sex Songs* playlist.

As R. Kelly's, *Honey Love* began to command the suite, Mystro started her seduction. She slowly walked over to the area in front of the couch, where Denver sat in anticipation, and kicked off her routine by lip-syncing to the song.

♪ *"Yeah come inside, now turn the lights down"*♪

♪ *"Don't be scared, touch me, I know what you want and uh"* ♪

♪ *"Tonight is your night, for the rest of your life"* ♪

♪ *"So just lay back and, relax and listen"* ♪

Mystro continued to mouth the words of the song while undressing herself to the beat. With each movement she made, she kept her eyes locked onto her target.

Denver sat on the edge of the couch grinding her body to the beat completely under Mystro's seductive spell.

"Mystro," Denver whispered, "I've seen you at the club so many times and I can't believe you are here with me."

"Shhhh, ma. No words need to be said now." Mystro was now down to her black wife beater and Polo boxer briefs. And for this dance, she was asked to bring her sex sidekick…her rubber dick. She wore the strap-on underneath her briefs already in place for action.

"Oh my God, Mystro, please fuck me," Denver called out while going under her negligee, revealing her red crouch-less thongs, and sliding her index finger into her warm pussy. She began to finger herself repeatedly, taking her drenched finger out occasionally to flick across her clit. "I want you so bad."

"Here I come, baby," Mystro answered while heading toward the couch, yanking off her boxer briefs on the way.

In anticipation, Denver pulled her legs up onto the couch and scooted to lie on her back. Mystro climbed over top of her and spread Denver's legs open to receive her pipe. Before she went to work, she kissed Denver passionately on her neck. Denver melted under Mystro's body. Mystro slid down to Denver's breasts and released them both from the negligee's hold. She sucked on her erect nipple's sending tiny shivers throughout Denver's body. The foreplay was nice and very seductive, but Mystro knew it was time to go to work.

"You ready," she asked while Denver continued to breathe heavy. She grabbed at the shaft of her dick. Mystro guided the tip of the head towards Denver's awaiting pussy. She rubbed the tip against her clit repeatedly to ensure her pussy was soaked before sliding inside her.

"Don't tease me, Mystro, fuck me, please." Denver screamed out.

Mystro obliged. Without further delay, she stuffed all eight inches of the dick into her pussy with her right hand, while gripping Denver's arms above her head with her left hand.

"Mmmmmmm…mmmmm, Mystro," Denver continued to scream out in ecstasy, while Mystro whined her waist and sexed her as if the rubber dick was a part of her own body. She fucked Denver with precision as she moved slowly, sliding in and out of her.

"Ah…ah…ah," was the only thing Denver could say as she received the fuck of her life. The fuck she longed for.

"Turn over, I gotta hit this ass from the back," Mystro demanded as she lifted her body up to allow Denver to flip over.

Denver turned onto her knees and maneuvered her body to lie face down on the couch. Her upper torso was lowered and her ass was hiked so far into the air, it could touch the ceiling. Mystro grabbed onto the top of her ass and pushed it upward, exposing her open pussy. She walked into her pussy on her knees and inserted her dick slowly into Denver.

"Ahhhhhhhhhhhhh…mmmmmmmm," Denver moaned as she whined her waist and pumped back into Mystro, taking all that she had to give.

Once Mystro got her rhythm, there was no stopping her. She banged Denver's thick ass as if she was beefing with her. She remained speechless as Mystro spanked her ass cheeks while pounding her pussy. Denver experienced orgasm after orgasm, as Mystro found her G-spot and tapped it with accuracy. Within fifteen minutes, Denver's legs began to shake as she screamed out her third orgasm. Mystro outdid herself and she knew it.

"You want something to drink," Mystro asked as she pulled herself off of Denver's ass and onto her feet to walk over to the bar. She grabbed her boxer briefs from the floor on the way and slid them up over her harnessed dick. She had not adjusted it so the rubber dildo poked her boxers outward making her appear as if she had a hard dick ready for round two.

"You were everything I fantasized you to be," Denver said as she grabbed the water bottle from Mystro and took a sip. Mystro didn't say anything; she began to gather her clothes off the floor to get dressed. Denver noticed Mystro was prepared to leave but did not want the night to end yet. "Mystro, I would love for you to stay the night with me. I mean…I'll pay."

"I appreciate it, ma, really I do, but I gotta get home."

Mystro, now fully dressed, walked back towards the bar to unplug her iPod. She came, she saw and she conquered, and now it was time to bounce.

Denver swung her legs down off the couch and sat up.

"Mystro, I want you to stay, what can I say to make you," she asked.

"I'm sorry, ma I had fun too, but I really do have to press, take care." She turned and walked towards the door to make her exit.

"I'll pay you triple your fee," Denver yelled out.

With her back toward Denver and her hand on the doorknob, Mystro stopped and paused on her last statement. *'Triple'* she thought. She was already getting a thousand as her normal fee, but triple meant three thousand. She could get her condo a lot faster with that kind of money and move Church out of that nigga's house, and into a home of their own.

While Mystro fantasized in her head about living with Church permanently, Denver yelled out, "Everyone needs money for something. What do you need it for?"

# CHAPTER 22

Mystro picked up her homie Baby Dom, from her hang out, *All of the Lights Arcade* to ride with her to go condo shopping. They were at the third apartment building of the day and it looked like the best one was saved for last. With designated parking spaces, and a view of Southwest, Washington D.C.'s waterfront, Mystro believed she found her new place.

"Man, my boo gonna go off when she see this joint," Mystro said standing in front of the balcony door looking out onto the water. "I can't believe it didn't even take that long for me to get the scratch up to get into this spot."

Mystro thought about the job that started to bankroll her fund. She earned three thousand dollars for her time and attention in the Presidential Suites with Denver. Although she was apprehensive about staying the night at Denver's request, she knew she needed the money. Besides, when she called Church to tell her what the proposition was, Church told her she better get paid. Her exact words were, "Never leave the customer unsatisfied." So Mystro stayed and got her money, but hated how Church gave a fuck only about the ends and not the fact that her girl was staying out all night.

"Fam, I know you all sised and shit…'bout this living situation but shawty not gonna move in here with you," Baby Dom stated as she sat on the counter top of the kitchen's breakfast nook.

Mystro turned around to address her statement, "What you mean, slim?"

"I'm saying," Baby Dom jumped down off the counter and approached Mystro "I learned two things growing up in group homes. One, was to recognize when I met real, genuine peeps. And I knew I was good at it the day I met you and Native. And two, I learned to recognize a snake, like I saw when I met your girl, Church. She's not good enough for you, My. She gonna get you into trouble, I can feel it."

Mystro turned back around to look out the patio window while she still listened to Baby Dom. "You speaking out of turn, BD."

"Look, you and Native are the only true people I call family. Ya'll have looked out for me more than anyone has my whole life. It ain't shit I wouldn't do for ya'll, that's why I gotta keep it all the way one hundred with you, cuz I love you. Church, is on some different shit and if I were you, I would leave her ass alone." Baby Dom looked up to Mystro for her response.

"Baby Dom, I 'preciate you getting that off your chest, I know that was hard for you," Mystro turned to look down at her. "Not for nothing though,

but you too young to know 'bout love. And sometimes when people are in love, they argue, fight and
do crazy shit. And what me and Church got is love.
Ya'll just don't understand her. She really is a beautiful person inside and out. Ya'll prolly don't even
know that she volunteer's to teach inner city youth
girls ballet do you? That's out the kindness of her
heart, she don't get paid to do that." Mystro defended.

"Naw, I ain't know that." Baby Dom admitted.

"I bet. Look, I been doing these wild ass gigolo
jobs and been stacking my bread, and that was her
and my agreement; so she *will* be moving in here,
trust me. Truth be told, you prolly just pissed cuz she
caught you stealing."

"What," Baby Dom asked in shock.

"Yeah, Church told me that the night we did
the debut of our new show, she caught you trying to
pocket fifty bucks."

"Man, I ain't take no money from ya'll," Baby
Dom yelled. "I would never steal from you, Fam."

Mystro whipped her neck around quick to face
her like someone tapped her on the shoulder and
said, "Get the fuck outta here, are you forgetting the
Jordan's you lifted and the money you spent of ours
the first time we danced?" Mystro laughed.

"You know I was on some different shit when I
took them shoes. My mental was still on self. Far as
the money is concerned," she paused, "I just got

caught up in the bitches, but you know I paid that back…in full and haven't so much as lifted a piece of lint from ya'll."

"Look, it's cool, I'm not stunting that, just fall back. Me and Church are gonna be together, she gonna move in here with me and soon we gonna get married and I'd really appreciate it if you and Native would just except that shit." Mystro was agitated. "You say you love me, so just be happy for me."

—  ▪  —  ▪  —  ▪  —  ▪  —  ▪  —  ▪  —

Baby Dom walked down the street that led to Church's house. Mystro getting serious with Church, and trying to move her in a condo was eating at her. She needed to check this broad out on her own and see what she was all about.

As she rounded the corner two houses up from Church's, she had to dive behind a Ford pick up truck when she saw Church's door open. She watched as Church stepped out while on her cell phone and closed the door behind her. She headed towards her BMW. But before she could get into her car, the house door opened back up and a bare chest dude, who wore blue basketball shorts and slippers only, came out the house carrying a pink gym bag. Baby Dom crouched lower behind the blue pickup's flatbed and took in the scene.

"Baby, how you gonna teach your class without your stuff," the dude handed Church her gym bag. "You lucky I caught you before you left for work."

"Wow, I'm tripping, thank you, sweetie," Church said as she ended her call and walked back towards the dude to retrieve her bag. She stood up on her tiptoes and gave him a kiss before she continued. "Don't forget to lock the top lock when you leave the house. I'll call you after I meet with Mystro."

"Don't sugar coat the shit, Church," the dude said angrily, "you going on a date with that dyke. How much longer you gotta do this shit? I think this one is going too far. It feels different from the others."

Church placed her bag inside her open car and turned back around to face the dude. She wrapped her arms around his waist and looked up into his eyes and said, "Gee, what has gotten into you? This is what we do, you know that. Do you feel threatened by a female or something?"

"Girl, you want me to choke you out here," dude threatened looking dead in her eyes. "Fuck no I ain't threatened by no bitch. I'm a man. She can't give you what I can, and you and I both know that."

"Then why you doing the most? I mean that whole showing up at the gym and getting into it with her in the parking lot was way over the top. You played yourself. I thought you blew it for us. Keep your feelings under control, I'm always gonna be yours."

"Yeah, but I didn't fuck it up. So how much longer you got with her anyway," Dude asked.

"Oh, I know what it is, this is the first time I have ever been with a Dom and you can't handle it, huh." Church teased. "You like the soft and feminine ones, who are fuckable to you."

Dude looked away and flexed his jaws while sighing.

Church laughed. "Well, don't worry about it. Whether she's fem or dom, it's all money for us. Be patient, baby, they are getting us paid. I already got them heavy into the fucking part of the plan, so just a little bit longer and we out, and on to the next flunkies. Don't worry, she won't steal me away from you," she laughed and puckered up for another kiss. This time the kiss was deep and passionate. Dude reached down and cupped Church's ass while he slid his tongue into her mouth strongly.

Church pulled away. "Baby, I gotta go and you trying to get something started."

"Five minutes, come on," Dude begged pulling at the erection in his shorts.

Church grabbed his dick, kicked her car door shut and led him back into the house and slammed the door.

—■·—·—·—·—·—·—·—■

"I knew that broad was on some crab shit," Baby Dom said to herself still staring at the house. I'm gonna get that sneaky bitch if it's the last thing I do."

# CHAPTER 23

Baby Dom stood on the outside of Native and Mystro's house holding a large pizza and a twelve pack of canned Budweiser's. She had an eventful day and just wanted to be around her homies. She sat the beer down and banged on the wooden door.

"Slim, why we gotta tell you every time to stop banging on this door," Mystro said. She snatched the door open to let Baby Dom in before she walked away.

"I be wanting to make sure ya'll hear me, Fam, that's all. My bad," she said as she picked up the beer, and stepped into the house. Once inside she turned and closed the door.

"I made sure that I came correct, I hope ya'll hungry," Baby Dom yelled awkwardly, while she sat the stuff down on the coffee table and walked to a chair. Native sat up from her slouched position on the couch and opened the box of canned beer to grab one.

"Hell yeah, I was just saying I was starving, this right on time, slim." Native stated while she reached for a slice of pizza.

Mystro walked the box of her belongings that she held in her arms, near the door, and approached the table of food and drink.

Baby Dom sat on the opposite side of the room. She appeared to be off in her head and deep in thought. She positioned herself in the living room chair shaking her leg.

"BD, why you over there looking crazy?" Native asked observing the awkward behavior she displayed.

"Huh," she said snapping out of her thought. "Oh, I'm cool...hey did ya'll see that game?" Baby Dom asked out of nowhere trying to spark conversation and take the eyes off her.

"What game are you talking about, kid? Skins ain't play today." Native replied staring her down as if she was trying to see through her. "Fuck is wrong with you? You must've got into some shit huh?"

"More than you know, Fam," she eluded the question and shook off her thoughts. "It ain't nothing though, really, just had some broad that was fucking with me in my head, but it's cool now. What ya'll been up to?" She asked avoiding giving more detail about her issue.

Mystro shook her head and gulped down her beer. "We need to go fuck some folks up or what?" Mystro asked.

"Oh naw, Fam. I took care of it already. Shouldn't be no more issues." Baby Dom smirked.

"Well, we ain't doing shit in here...I'm just watching this fake ass Martha Stewart ass nigga get her stuff together to pack. You know she about to move into her crib," Native said smartly before she took a bite of her pizza.

"She don't need to be packing nothing yet," Baby Dom said under her breath. "If I were her I'd slow my roll...all the way down."

"I heard you lil nigga, I told you about hating on my boo too," Mystro scolded. Baby Dom rolled her eyes.

"Son, I can't believe your pussy whipped ass is really trying to leave the crib, this is the bachelor pad." Native proclaimed.

Mystro gave her a look over top of her beer can before she asked, "You joking right?"

"I'm serious as shit, I mean I can't fathom why the fuck you wanna roll out of our spot here to shack up with that bitch." Native asked with venom.

Mystro slammed her beer down on the table and yelled, "I told you not to call her that. You gonna make me hurt you, Native. I'm serious."

"Call 'em like I see 'em," Native yelled back. "She a bitch and you a fool for still fucking with her."

"Say that shit to my face." Mystro stepped up and stood over top of Native who still sat on the couch. If she said the wrong thing she was prepared to fight her like a nigga off of the street.

Native leaped up and matched Mystro's stance before she yelled, "I said you's a fucking –"

Mystro cocked back to hit her best friend in the face, when Baby Dom jumped up and ran toward them to break it up. "Whoa, Fam what ya'll doing," she asked grabbing Mystro's arm. Native stood in a defensive stance ready to block Mystro's punch.

"Get off me, Baby Dom," Mystro yelled snatching her arm from Baby Dom's grasp.

"Calm down, Mystro. We shouldn't be coming undone over some bit'--" Baby Dom stopped herself from calling Church a bitch too. Mystro turned her angered look towards Baby Dom. "I meant we shouldn't be fighting over some female...female." Baby Dom finished, while she held her hands in front of her in a defensive mode.

While the tension remained in the air, there was a loud knock at the door. Mystro turned away from Baby Dom and walked over to answer the knock.

"Church," Mystro said shocked, "what are you doing here?" She let her in.

"Uh...I gotta bounce," Baby Dom said when she saw Church coming in the door.

"Fuck no, slim, you ain't gotta go nowhere. This my house. Chill out," Native said with her arm on Baby Dom's shoulder to hold her back. Just then, she noticed a scent she hadn't smelled before and knew immediately it was Baby Dom. "Why you smell like gas," Native asked her in a whisper.

"Oh, uh, the car I was in ran out and I had to go get some more with a gas can. It spilled all over my feet." Baby Dom explained before staring at Mystro and Church.

"Babes, you don't look so good. Everything alright," Mystro asked Church still standing near the front door.

"No, there was a fire at my house, Mystro."

"A fire, what…how?"

"The fire department is not sure yet. But they are looking at possible arson." Church explained with a tear in her eye. Native looked back at Baby Dom.

"I'm so sorry, shawty," Mystro said pulling Church into a warm embrace. "I'm glad you got out ok. I would've killed somebody if something happened to you."

"No, I wasn't even home at the time. I was just coming back from class when I pulled up on the scene. The house was already in flames. I have no idea what I'm gonna do now, it completely burned down, I lost everything."

"Church, I know it's kinda fucked up, but it may be a sign. Look," Mystro pulled back from the hug and walked over to the stairs and grabbed a folder.

"Open it," she told Church as she stood back in front of her and handed her the folder.

"Mystro…it's a lease," Church looked at the contract in shock.

"Yep, I mean it ain't a condo, but it has a view of the water and it's all ours," she said while she reached into her sweatpants and pulled out the keys. "We moving in tonight, I gotta get outta here, anyway." Mystro continued looking back at Native who just stared on in anger and sadness.

# CHAPTER 24

Mystro was in her new apartment where she prepared a home-cooked meal for her and Church. It had been two weeks since Church's house burned down and they moved in together. Mystro was disappointed, the experience had not been the complete bliss she thought it would be living with her boo. All Church did was book dates for her and Native while she focused on the money. They only had sex once since they moved in, and Mystro was beyond frustrated.

"Hey, do you want any garlic bread," Mystro yelled from the kitchen where she cooked their dinner, Shrimp Alfredo. "It's ready."

Church didn't respond.

Mystro walked to the kitchen door and looked out of it to see why Church did not answer. She found her sitting in the living room wearing a pair of pink boy shorts, a white wife beater and no bra. As usual her head was buried into her laptop.

"Church," she called out again, "did you hear what I asked?"

"Huh, oh no, what," she replied never looking up from the computer screen. Mystro annoyed her. "What you want?"

"I asked if you wanted garlic bread with your pasta," Mystro repeated. She hated when Church ignored her and lately she had been doing that often.

"Ummm, no." Church noticed an incoming call on her cell phone. She answered it but did not say more than two words during the entire conversation, as if she was talking in code. Although she did not say much on the call, her facial expressions indicated that whatever she was being told had her pissed.

"Are you sure it was her," Church said into her phone. "How do you know?"

Mystro tried to ear hustle but her attempt failed. When Church ended her call, Mystro asked, "Who was that?"

Church looked up from her computer and stared directly at Mystro with heat in her eyes as if she did something to her. "What is your problem? I mean, why are you asking about who calling my phone? Do I ask who it is when your friends call?"

"No, my bad, baby, I just thought it might have been a job or something."

"Well, it wasn't. And speaking of your friends, where is Baby Dom? I haven't heard you talk about her much lately."

"She prolly on the block or hanging with Native, why you ask?" Mystro walked back and forth, while bringing the food out to the table.

"No reason really, she just crossed my mind, that's all." Church lied.

Mystro shrugged it off and sat at the table, "The food ready, baby, come eat."

"In a second, I just got two more bookings for you. One is a request for you and Native, and it's worth a lot of money."

Mystro looked up from blessing her food with concern. "Me and Native? As in going on a job together," she asked. "What kinda freaky shit is that? I ain't 'bout to be in some wild ass threesome with my best friend, well...ex-best friend." Mystro shoved a fork full of pasta in her mouth angrily. Her and Native hadn't spoken since the beef and she missed her.

"Oh yes you will too, if they paying," Church said in her dictator's voice that she was famous for. Mystro continued to eat in anger with her nostrils flared. "But don't worry your neat little cornrows, it's not just one girl, it's three and they paying for a private dance only."

"Yeah, well, I don't know 'bout all that. Me and Native ain't vibing too tough right now. I don't know if she trying to go on no jobs with me, and I feel the same way."

"Listen," Church said standing up to face Mystro. "I am not out here busting my ass to get bookings, just for you two bitches to get in ya'll feelings and fuck my money up. Now whatever problems ya'll got with each other, fix 'em because you *will* be working this party." She finished with her hands on her hips waiting on a response.

Mystro continued to stab at the food on her plate with anger. "Shawty, how long do we gotta do this shit for anyway? I'm saying, we got the apartment, the bills are paid and I even got almost fifteen stacks saved in our room. I'm trying to do something different with my life, and for my family. I was thinking about going to culinary school, I mean, I do like to cook. Maybe I can make it a career." She smiled.

"Culinary school…that's the dumbest thing I ever heard you say out your mouth," Church started. "In case you didn't know, school cost money and just where do you think you will get that money from?"

"I just said I got savings, and it don't cost that much."

"You are a fucking idiot, it's school, it does cost that much. And just what kind of family do you think you will be supporting? It can't be me."

"What you mean, I'm supporting you now ain't I?" Mystro yelled into her feelings.

"No, boo, don't get it twisted, I made you, and I book your shows and dates to get you paid. Therefore, I own you. I'm supporting you." Church stared at Mystro and waited for her comment. There wasn't one.

"You must not get what the fuck I been trying to tell you from the start," Church informed. "Sit right there," she continued as she left the dining room and dashed to the back of the apartment.

Mystro stopped eating her dinner. She sat in silence awaiting her return.

When Church came back into the room, she held a tan shoebox in her hands. She sat the box on top of an empty white plate on the table across from Mystro. She took off the top and removed a black stiletto shoe with a red bottom. "This is a Christian Louboutin stiletto. It retails at fourteen hundred dollars, US dollars. This is a simple black pump, but some of this designer's shoes cost several thousand dollars a pair. I only wear the finest in clothes, shoes and handbags. And that little bit of savings that you have would only provide me with half a day of shopping, maybe." She shrugs. "If I'm lucky." She placed the shoe back in the box and replaced the top.

"Church, I get that, I'm just saying –"

"You talking about caring for your family by quitting the one thing that is bringing you steady income," she cut her off. "Get real. You need to work this shit as long as you can while you still young and fine and bitches still want you. Because trust me, it won't always be the case. And when you got close to a million dollars saved up, come back and holla at me about quitting. Then you can go off and learn to cook pancakes, pastas, pies or whatever the hell you want."

Without another word, Church picked up her box and walked out of the dining room, leaving Mystro looking stupid.

# CHAPTER 25

Mystro sat in her car outside of Native's house where she waited on her so they could go to their scheduled booking. She had not seen her since the night of their argument, where she almost hit her with a closed fist. She hated how things were left between them. They had never had an argument of this magnitude and it weighed heavily on her. Not just because of the break in the friendship, but because she was starting to think Native was right about Church. But she loved her and was torn.

"What's up, son," Native said after she opened the car door and slid into the passenger seat.

"What up, champ," Mystro shot back while Native shut her door. There was awkward silence as Mystro drove off towards their destination.

"Thanks for coming to get me," Native said breaking the silence.

"No problem."

"Mystro, look, I'm sorry about last time," Native jumped out and apologized first. "I mean regardless of how I feel about Church, she ain't my girl. I shouldn't have called her out of her name."

"You know what, slim," Mystro said looking straight out onto the road while piloting her car through the dark and chilly DC streets. "You always been upfront 'bout not fucking with her. I shouldn't have gotten that pissed…you my family. I'm sorry for trying to swing on you. You got your opinions on the matter and I got mine. So, we cool?" Mystro held her right fist up towards Native.

Native held her left fist up and gave Mystro a pound. "Yeah, we boys again."

"Bet, let's go get this money."

■ ▪ ■ ▪ ■ ▪ ■ ▪ ■ ▪ ■ ▪ ■

Mystro and Native stood at the hotel door waiting for their clients to let them inside the room. After what seemed like only thirty seconds, the door swung open and a beautiful Brazilian looking woman stood on the other side.

"Brisa," Native said before stepping through the door. She had not seen or talked to her since she first met her in the mall parking lot before her and Mystro's failed caper.

"Hi, Native," she replied with a smile that lit up the room. "Come on in, we have been waiting on you all night."

"So, you knew it was me coming," Native asked still in shock.

"Well, I figured it had to be, how many sexy Dom's do you meet with a unique name like Native?" Brisa laughed. "You must be Mystro." She extended her hand for a shake.

"Yes, I am, pleased to meet you." Mystro shook Brisa's hand.

"Damn, how did you hear about us," Native asked.

"My friend actually was the one who brought it up and booked you guys."

"Where are your friends? We were told this was a three person request for a private dance." Mystro stated.

"Oh, she's coming, she's in the other room, but it's just her and I. Our other girl chickened out. She was afraid her son's father was going to find out and go off." Brisa informed.

When the bedroom door opened, Mystro could not believe who entered the living room area of the suite looking sexy and seductive.

"Breezy," both she and Native screamed. Mystro was in shock as she looked into the eyes of her friend that used to keep her braids tight.

"Hey, boo," Breezy yelled as she ran up to Mystro for a hug. Mystro held her arms opened and when Breezy slid inside them, she scooped her up into an embrace.

"How do ya'll two know each other," Mystro asked Brisa while she maintained her grip on Breezy.

"Oh we go way back, Breezy and me. We work together at the salon," Brisa offered.

"Yo, this is so corny," Native yelled and laughing hysterically. "This is like some shit you would see in the movies or read in a book. This kinda stuff don't happen in real life."

"Native, you still the same I see," Breezy said breaking away from Mystro and turning towards Native for a hug.

"You know me, ma," Native shot back while she gripped Breezy in a one armed embrace. "I do a lot but I never change."

"So, this little reunion of ours is cute, but when does the show get started?" Brisa asked.

Mystro and Native looked at each other. "Whenever ya'll ready. How do you wanna do it?" Mystro asked.

"Well, since it's my birthday, I want to have a private, private dance," Breezy said. She grabbed Mystro's hand. "Plus, I don't want to see Native gyrating all over the place. No offense, Nae." Breezy said laughing.

"No, sweat. I work better alone anyway," Native replied eyeing Brisa.

Breezy escorted Mystro into the bedroom of the suite and closed the door. When she entered, she noticed there was Dom Perignon champagne, along with a fruit, cracker and cheese platter, sitting on the desk. Breezy released Mystro's hand and sat on the edge of the King sized bed after she closed the door.

"So, should I sit here or in the desk chair," Breezy asked looking up at Mystro.

"Hold up, shawty. I gotta know how you found out we danced?" Mystro said sitting in the desk chair across from her.

"Well," she started, "so much has happened in the months since I last saw you. First, I moved out of Kenilworth to Mitchellville Maryland."

"Good," Mystro said happily. "I'm so happy you not 'round there no more. You know the last time I came through I got stuck up?"

"Noooo, Mystro, why didn't you tell me?"

"Cuz, what could you have done? I ain't wanna get you involved no way, you had to live over there still."

"Is that why you hadn't called me to get your hair done, although I see somebody been keeping you tight." Breezy said with slight attitude.

Mystro laughed and ran her hand over her braids. "Yes and no, I mean I kinda got caught up in one thing after another right after that." She continued looking away from Breezy. "Can I pop open this champagne?" Mystro swung the chair around and grabbed the bottle to open it.

"Absolutely, let's get this party started." Breezy moved her waist from side to side in a seated dance motion on the bed. "So, what's her name?" She stopped dancing.

"Huh?"

"Mystro, I've known you for a little while now, and it's one thing I know for sure, when you have a chick, you go all in. Sometimes too much, so what's her name?"

"I don't wanna talk about her, if it's aight with you." Breezy nodded in agreement. "Good, now back to you. So you moved, but you still haven't told me how you heard about us." Mystro poured the champagne.

"Oh, right, so I'm in the shop working one day and I overhear my client on a call. She said she couldn't wait until her date. She said she heard that Mystro was the bomb and she was long overdue for some special attention."

Mystro looked into her cup ashamed of what she did to earn a living. "Look, Breezy, ummm, I'm only doing this shit for a little while. I mean, I got plans."

"Don't be embarrassed, Mystro. I truly believe everything happens for a reason. Besides, if you didn't provide this service, how else would I have gotten to partake?" Breezy sipped her drink.

"Stop playing, shawty, you on dick. You not into bitches." Mystro downed the champagne in her cup.

"No, I'm not into bitches, you right about that," Breezy advised, "but I am into you."

■ ▪ ■ ▪ ■ ▪ ■ ▪ ■ ▪ ■

In the living room, *Wicked Games* by The Weekend was heard coming from Native's plugged in iPod. She just wrapped up her dance session for Brisa. They were now standing locked in a passionate kiss. That is until Native broke out of it.

"Damn, ma, you move quick. I thought I was supposed to be seducing you," Native said confused.

"You did, that's why I can't keep my hands off you," Brisa said pressing her C cup breasts up against Native's chest. Brisa took charge and normally, Native hated for girls to do that. But for some reason she was turned on by her display of aggression.

"I have been thinking about you ever since the day you harassed me in that parking lot," Brisa advised.

"Oh yeah, well why you ain't call me then?"

"I was waiting on you. You never called either, Native."

Native was embarrassed and debated whether or not she would tell her the real reason she never called. *'Fuck it'*, she thought as she began to spill the beans. "If I tell you why, you better not laugh," Native advised seriously.

"I'm listening," Brisa said staring into Native's eyes.

Native looked away from her and said, "I was nervous. I ain't know what to say to you if I called."

.

"You did ok in the parking lot, why would it be any different?"

"Man, I don't know. I ain't never been nervous 'bout no female and you gave me butterflies, even then. I was just trying to play it off. You are stunning, ma." Native looked into Brisa's eyes.

Brisa blushed, "I do have one question though, how did you know I was in the life?"

"I didn't, but I had to take a chance." Native confessed.

Brisa smiled. "See, that wasn't so bad, right? You can be honest with me. I'm still just a girl, Native, and I'm very attracted to you." She moved in for another kiss. As Brisa pulled away from her lip lock, she said, "now, I know we paid for ya'll, but I'm in the mood to serve. Will you let me?"

"What you talking 'bout, girl?"

Without words Brisa squatted down and got on her knees. She grabbed at Native's black Louis Vuitton belt and yanked it open. She proceeded to unbutton her jeans and pulled them, along with her Polo boxers, down to her ankles.

"Brisa, what you doing," Native asked still standing with her back to the wall, looking at her pants being snatched down.

"I'm getting ready to make you feel incredible." She said grabbing the back of Native's thighs and placing her mouth up over Native's clit before she could refuse.

"SSSSS…ahhhh," Native yelled out in ecstasy, as Brisa gave her head standing up. Native's mind was spinning. No broad had ever done this to her before. She was being turned out and she loved it.

"Fuckkkkkkk," Native shouted out as she gripped the back of Brisa's hair and tugged it gently while pumping her waist into her every lick and suck. When Brisa pawed Native's ass and bared down over her clit while sucking it at the same time, Native couldn't take it anymore and bust her nut onto Brisa's tongue.

Brisa stopped, wiped her mouth with the back of her hand then stood up and kissed Native with vigor. When they broke from the kiss, Brisa said, "I bet you gonna call me now."

# CHAPTER 26

Mystro walked up the hallway steps leading to her apartment and she wore a huge smile on her face. It was seven o'clock in the morning and she was just getting home from the date Church sent her on, that ended up being a reunion for her and Native, and she felt different. She reached her apartment door and before she could put the key in the lock, Church snatched it open wearing a pink terrycloth robe and her hair was up in a silk leopard print bonnet.

"Where the fuck have you been," Church spat with venom.

"What you talking 'bout, shawty?" Mystro strolled inside the apartment and past Church.

"You know exactly what I'm talking about, Mystro. Where have you been all fucking night?" Church slammed the apartment door and ran behind Mystro who headed straight for the kitchen.

"I was at the hotel," she said drinking orange juice straight out of the carton, while standing in front of the refrigerator. "On the date you sent me to." Mystro closed the fridge door and stared down into Church's eyes.

"Bullshit, that bitch paid for a private dance from Hersband Material and that's it. You should have been done with them thirty minutes after you got there."

"Wasn't it you that told me never leave the customer un-satisfied?"

Church stared Mystro up and down before responding. "I did, so where's the money she gave you for your extra time?"

Mystro sat the orange juice carton down on the counter and attempted to walk out of the kitchen. Church blocked her path. "Baby, I don't have any additional money. I just stayed-"

"Don't baby me, why would you stay and not get paid," Church yelled up at Mystro.

She paused before she answered her. She really didn't feel like arguing and she knew that is where her answer would lead. But she had no choice. "I knew her, Church, aight. I knew her and Native knew her friend. So we just kicked it with them for her birthday. Before I knew it, the sun was coming up."

"Oh, them bitches tried it. Had I known you knew 'em I wouldn't have booked that shit." Church ranted.

"Why not, money is money right? What difference does it make?" She said feeding Church back her own philosophy.

"Don't play with me, Mystro. Your time is money and if the bitch wanted more of your time, she should have paid the money. I gotta good mind to call her right now and let her know she owes me." Church headed to her laptop to retrieve Breezy's information.

"It ain't that deep, shawty. The mistake was mine, so I'll give you your fee." Mystro walked towards the bedroom.

Church was speechless and pissed. She should be happy, since all she cared about was the all mighty dollar, but she wasn't. For a brief moment she felt their relationship was real and Mystro disrespected her. She forgot that she truly did not give a fuck, because maybe she was starting to care. And it made her angrier that Mystro seemed to not give a fuck. Something was different with her and Church knew it.

So she followed behind her to the room. "When are you giving me my money?"

"Church, look I'm tired. All I want to do is get in the shower and lay down. We can pick this up later if you want." Mystro emptied her pockets and placed the contents on the dresser. She took off her clothes and put them in the hamper for the cleaners before she headed to the shower.

Church stood in the bedroom fuming and in a daze. It wasn't until she heard Mystro's cell phone beep, indicating she had a text message that she snapped out of her haze of anger. She waited until she heard the water running in the shower before she ran over to the dresser and picked up Mystro's phone. The message was from Breezy and it read,

**Thanx 4 staying with me. U made my Bday the best ;)**

Church was heated. *'Horny ass bitch. Can't keep shit professional'* She thought. She deleted the message and proceeded to find the applications store on Mystro's iPhone. When she found it, she searched for the app called *Friend Locate*. A grin covered her face as she pushed the button to purchase it. Looking back at the bathroom door, she quickly installed the app on Mystro's phone and approved the request from her own phone. This handy feature would allow Church to track Mystro's whereabouts at all times.

Placing Mystro's phone back on the dresser she whispered, "Now, wherever you go, I'll know exactly where you are."

# CHAPTER 27

"Two more buckets and that's game, son," Native yelled out after making her shot. She and Mystro were on the outdoor basketball court playing a game of one-on-one in Native's neighborhood.

"Not if I get my basket first, champ," Mystro replied, attempting to strip the ball from Native's grasp.

"Ha ha too slow," Native laughed while moving the ball out of Mystro's reach. "I ain't even think you was gonna show up out here today. Being as though you ain't get much sleep last night while you were in there with Breezy, I just knew you was gonna be in for the day." Native dribbled the ball and tried to drive the lane past Mystro towards the hoop.

"Naw, I had to get outta that apartment. Church in there pissed cuz I stayed out all night."

Native frowned. "Why she tripping? You stayed out all night with a client before right?"

"Yeah, but I also brought home three stacks for that. I ain't bring shit home this time," Mystro explained. "She ain't stupid."

Native shook her head. "She'll be aight man. What I need to know is if you hit or not?"

"Come on, slim you know it wasn't that type of party. They just paid for the dance."

"I don't give a fuck what they paid for, I wanna know did you get down?"

Mystro laughed trying to avoid the question. "What about you? Brisa bad as shit, slim. I know you had to taste that."

"Hey, son, you not gonna believe it even though I'm telling you," Native took a shot at the hoop and missed. Mystro grabbed the rebound. "She posted me up on the wall, got on her knees, snatched my pants down and went to work. And it was the best head I ever had...in my life."

"What," Mystro yelled. "She sucked your dick, Native, damn! Did you at least dance for her?"

"Yeah, man, I danced and then she jumped on me, tongued me down, then dropped to her knees and tongued me down there. And...I think I'm in love."

Mystro stopped dribbling the ball and bent over in laughter. Native never caught feelings.

"Yeah, I said it, fuck it. That girl 'bout to make me cut my roster down, slim, real shit." Mystro cracked up. "Enough about that though, what Breezy taste like?"

Mystro stood up and debated whether or not she wanted to tell Native the truth. "Aight" – she started while taking her final game winning shot and making it – "We ain't get down all like that, but we did get intimate –"

"I knew it," Native yelled cutting Mystro off. She grabbed the ball, and stuffed it under her arm. "How'd it feel?"

"To be honest, it felt good. I mean I always thought Breezy was sexy and flirtatious with me, but I never thought I had a chance. She was on dick too hard."

"You know how many broads I turned out, Mystro? Too many to name or remember. Her being on dick don't mean shit. She always flirted with you on the low…hard! She was prolly just waiting on you to make a move. But, for real, since you used to be that *stalking type motherfucka* for these bitches out here, I'm kinda glad it worked out like this. It gave you time to grow," Native schooled.

Mystro frowned. "Look, I was never the stalking type, Native."

"You playing right?"

"I'm dead serious. I was in love back then, and the shit wasn't being returned. In my opinion it wasn't me, it was them."

Native shook her head. "It's one thing to love somebody, Mystro, and another thing to push yourself onto somebody who don't want you back. I'ma be real with you. Just be glad you seeing straight now. This shit between you and Breezy seems destined, and you shouldn't fuck it up."

Mystro didn't like being thought of as a stalker, but she did understand where Native was coming from too. "I don't know about that destiny shit, but I am feeling her. And Breezy jive said something along those lines too. She said everything happens for a reason, which I'm really starting to believe. I still feel bad though, about Church. That's my girl and regardless of what problems we may have, I shouldn't have cheated on her. This move don't sit right with me."

"Do you hear yourself," Native asked, "your so called girl sent you out on that date. Shit, she's sent you on several fucking dates. You've had sex with a bunch of bitches who she found. So what you enjoyed yourself a little with Breezy. That's your noble right."

"Yeah, but with all them other broads, it was work. This shit with Breezy felt different. I couldn't stop thinking about her. Then I came in the house and Church jumped down my throat. She was burnt up, son."

"I don't feel sorry for her at all. It's her own fault. She got us into this. Looks like the shit backfired on that ass if you ask me."

"Yeah, but now she don't trust me. She done put a tracking app on my phone and shit. I mean how dumb do she think I am that I wouldn't notice a new app? I mean it's my phone."

Before Native could reply, a neighborhood dude ran up on them at the court. "Say, where's ya'll little half-pint side kick at?" he asked.

"Who you talking 'bout, Cool, Baby Dom," Native questioned.

"Yeah, yeah, that's her."

"I don't know, I haven't seen her in a couple days. Why you ask?"

"Look, nigga's is looking for her. They saying she burnt down that pimp bitch and her man's house. They putting a few dollars on her head and every-thing."

"What, nigga, what pimp bitch you talking 'bout," Mystro asked him.

"A chick name Church, she live with her man uptown. They be setting dyke's up to pimp 'em out and get money off their work." Cool continued. He realized he was talking to two dykes, and that he might be a little offensive so he decided to cut his convo short. "Look, I ain't trying to start nothing. Just wanted to warn you to find your friend. The nigga just got straight out of the city hospital from his burn injury and he searching for her. When you find her, hide her," Cool finished before bouncing off just as fast as he came.

"Damn," Native yelled. "That's us, My. She been playing us. I knew it. This shit makes so much sense now."

"Come on, son, you gonna take the word of the neighborhood gossip? I don't believe him."

"Mystro, wake up. She been running game on us from the start. You got to be crazy if you don't see it, specially now."

Mystro was deep in her feelings. Lately, she had been feeling like Church was not all she was cracked up to be. But she couldn't admit it to herself. Now to be hearing this information about her made her feel somewhat used. But she wanted to still give Church the benefit of the doubt. After all, the source of the information was a drunk.

"Look, before we get into that bullshit about her probably pimping us or not, let's go find Baby Dom. Everything else can wait," Mystro said.

# CHAPTER 28

After driving around for most of the day, it finally dawned on Mystro and Native to check Baby Dom's usual hang out spots. They rolled past, *Star's Laser Tag* and she wasn't there. They ended up at *All of the Lights Arcade* and found her there trying to book a chick.

"So I'm saying, boo, you should let me go 'head and get that number. I be seeing how you watch me handle the ball in the shootout game. I know you feeling a nigga," Baby Dom said, spitting game to the teenage admirer.

"Excuse us, sweetheart," Mystro interrupted while she pulled Baby Dom away from the young girl. "We been looking all over for you, slim what you doing here?"

"What up, Fam, what you mean, I been chilling here like I usually do," Baby Dom replied. "Why you cock block my action though? I'm trying to hit shawty off right quick."

"BD, you ain't got time for no fucking, we gotta book. Folks got word out 'round the way that you was involved in some shit and they coming for you. They got a bounty on your lil ass, so we gotta get outta here." Native looked around the arcade. "This place ain't safe for you no more."

Mystro and Native snatched her by the arms without another word.

■ ▪ ■ ▪ ■ ▪ ■ ▪ ■ ▪ ■ ▪ ■ ▪ ■

"I ain't know where else to go, but we should be cool here," Mystro said looking out the window of the hotel room. "I mean even if Church tracks me, we not far from the apartment and I can shoot home quickly," Mystro explained. "So, Baby Dom, its time to anti up. What's going on, champ, why bammas looking for you about a fire?" Mystro asked intently.

Baby Dom sat in the desk chair in the middle of the room. Before she spoke, she looked at Native for re-assurance. "Go 'head, son, tell us what happened. We gotchu," Native advised, sitting on top of the desk while she drank a bottle of water.

Baby Dom took a deep breath and said, "Aight, after we was looking at the apartment talking about Church, I was jive burnt up. I went around where she lived and spied on her. I needed to try and get proof so Mystro could leave that bitch alone." Mystro and Native listened attentively. "When I got on her street, she was coming out the house, but she wasn't alone," she paused looking up at Native.

"Dog, keep going, she gotta hear this shit, however it sounds," Native coached. Mystro stood near the bottom of the bed motionless.

Baby Dom shook her head but kept going. "A nigga came out the house behind her. It was the same nigga I seen her give ya'll tip money to that night at the Delta."

"What slim look like," Native asked.

"Ole Kevin Hart looking motherfucka but taller and wit' a beard."

"My, that sounds like the nigga we was 'bout to wreck in the gym parking lot," Native insinuated looking at Mystro.

Mystro took a seat on the edge of the bed and said, "That don't mean she wit' the nigga, I mean he is her landlord."

"Naw, Fam, it was more than that. The nigga had on slippers and balling shorts that looked just like the Kevin Durant shorts you bought two weeks ago. And he ain't have no shirt on either. He was in chill mode, not landlord mode," Baby Dom continued.

"She got that bamma ass nigga wearing your shit," Native yelled heated. Mystro looked down at the floor and rolled her eyes.

"There's more," Baby Dom said sadly shaking her head from left to right, "they talked for a minute outside and it looked like they was arguing at first, I couldn't really hear what they said. But then they slobbed each other down right there for the whole neighborhood to see." She eluded the part where dude's erection made an appearance, right before they went back into the house to fuck. Baby Dom hated to tell this messy information to her friend, but she knew she needed to in order to get Mystro away from Church for good.

Mystro looked up at Native, then at Baby Dom and asked, "So you did it, you burned down they crib?"

"Yeah, I had to, you should've seen 'em, Mystro, I was so pissed. I was hoping I got they asses both while they was in there together. I wanted her out your life, but that shit backfired on me and she ended up having to move in with you." Baby Dom confessed.

"Well, apparently the nigga *was* in there when you lit it up. He been in the hospital this whole time for his injuries until recently. And now, he out and looking for you." Native jumped down off the desk and sat on the bed next to Mystro. "You see this bitch ain't no good now, son?"

"I just can't believe she would do some shit like that to me, why?" Mystro asked still in denial.

Native laid back on the bed and put her hands on the top of her head. "I can't believe you don't see this bitch is playing you," she sprang back up into a seated position and looked at Mystro. "What the fuck is it gonna take, do you need more proof?"

"Man, it ain't just that simple. I love this girl. I wanted to marry her. I can't just up and quit her like that. What about the life I'm building for the both of us? What about our family?"

"Hold up, you said *wanted* to marry her, so somewhere inside, you realize she may not be the one." Native shoved Mystro's own words back at her.

When she said she wanted to marry her, as to imply she felt differently now, things hit home. Mystro drifted out of the conversation. She thought back on the talk she had with Church the last night she cooked dinner. Mystro felt Church's intentions were only money driven then, whether she admitted it or not.

"Aight," she said with her head down on the verge of tears, "how do I find out for sure? That she's cheating?"

"Yes, finally," Native yells happily. "I think you need to set her up," she suggests.

"Yeah, see how she carry shit when you not around, only you show up, like I did. She bound to be doing some hot shit," Baby Dom added.

Mystro's phone rang while she was in deep contemplation. When she retrieved it out of her basketball shorts pocket, she saw Church's praying hands tattoo on the screen indicating she was calling.

"Hold up, don't say nothing, this her," Mystro said leaping off the bed and walking into the bathroom to take the call.

"Hello."

"Hey, baby, where are you," Church asked off the top.

"Not far from the crib, why what's up?"

"I was just trying to see what you were up to. I wanted to make this a date night, you know dinner and maybe a movie," Church responded. "You down?"

Mystro was shocked, in all the time they had been together Church rarely initiated a date night. She wondered what Church might be up too. She decided to test Native and Baby Dom's theory and set her up.

"Oh, damn, shawty, that would've been cool, but I'm getting ready to head out Bmore. A partner of mine having a bachelor party. I'ma be gone most of the night," Mystro lied as her stomach knotted.

"Ok, well have fun. Call me when you on your way home. I might want you to stop by and bring me something to eat," Church finished.

"Yeah, aight, I'll holla at you later." Mystro ended the call and leaned on the sink.

She couldn't believe it was a possibility that the woman she wanted to marry had been playing her from the start. She felt ill. She turned around and cut the cold water on to splash some on her face. When she was done, she dried off with a hand towel and looked at herself in the mirror.

"How come I can't catch a fucking break?" She said to her reflection. On the verge of tears, her thoughts wandered to Breezy. *'Could all this shit be happening to make an opening for her'*, she thought. She wasn't sure, but she knew she had to go through with this set up to know once and for all.

Mystro exited the bathroom to find her friends sitting in the same spots she left them waiting on her return.

"What it is, My," Native asked as Baby Dom looked on.

Mystro took a deep breath and said, "It's in motion, and now I need ya'll to carry out part two of my plan."

# CHAPTER 29
## THREE HOURS LATER

Mystro walked onto the street where her apartment was located. Her head was fucked up and her stomach felt like she drank some old milk. She knew that there was a possibility that in five minutes, she could be faced with what she was looking for. Evidence that Church had been just using her all along. She hoped all went well with the plan that she laid out to Mystro and Baby Dom, because she didn't have her cell phone to be reached on if it didn't.

Her plan consisted of Native and Baby Dom taking Mystro's car and driving out to Baltimore Maryland. She instructed Native to take her cell phone and dump it in the trashcan of the Hyatt Hotel on Light Street. That way if Church tried to find her location, she would think she really did go to a bachelor party, leaving her with plenty of time to do whatever she wanted free and clear, or so she thought. But the closer Mystro got to her building, the more she started to regret it all.

As she walked across the lawn of her complex, she glanced over into the designated parking spaces allotted for her apartment. She saw Church's car in it's space, but it was the car next to it, parked in

Mystro's space, that made her heartbeat increase. It was a gold Lexus, the same gold Lexus that Church's so called landlord jumped out of in the gym parking lot. Part of Mystro wanted to go back to the hotel and lie to Native and Baby Dom by telling them they were wrong about Church, and that nothing happened. But the other part knew she had to find out the truth. She took a deep breath to try and relieve the lump in her throat as she willed her feet to move forward.

She got up to her apartment and leaned into the door, to listen before entering. She could hear music faintly, and from the sounds of it, it appeared to be deep within the apartment. She deduced that it was probably being played in the bedroom, so she decided to creep in slowly.

Mystro placed her key into the lock and turned the knob gently. She leaned into the door and pushed it slightly so she could peek in first. When she got it open far enough, she stuck her head inside and scanned the living room. There was no one there. So she entered the apartment and closed the door softly behind her.

Walking through her living room, leading to her bedroom felt like she was walking to the electric chair. The clothes that were draped all over the floor served as a trail to the infidelity that was probably going on inside her bedroom. She paused herself in mid creep mode, to grab a knife out of the kitchen.

She didn't plan to use it, but if the same nigga was in her room, who she met before, she doubted their meeting would end well.

Mystro stood in the hallway directly in front of her bedroom door. She could clearly hear Miguel's song, *Pussy Is Mine*, bellowing throughout the room and Church moaning in the background. Suddenly, Mystro's sadness and nervousness turned into pure rage. She kicked in the bedroom door and saw her baby being plowed from behind by a set of dick and balls, *literally*.

She snapped.

Mystro charged at them and stabbed the nigga in the right shoulder.

"Aghhhhhhhhhh," he yelled out.

"Mystro, what the fuck are you doing here, you were just in Baltimore," Church screamed.

Mystro didn't address Church, she didn't take her eyes off the nigga. She moved to try and stab him again but this time he tucked his wounded shoulder and swung at her wildly with his left fist. He wild out so hard, that he missed Mystro and connected with Church's temple instead, knocking her out cold. He didn't so much as pause to check on her well-being as he leaped from the bed and came at Mystro full throttle with a hard wet dick and anger in his eyes. His shoulder was barely bleeding, like the nigga must have been part robot or something. He reached out to grab Mystro but she slipped his grasp and stuck him again, this time in his bandaged burnt thigh.

"Arrrghhhhhh," he growled as he grabbed at his thigh and turned around to escape her knifing fury. As he spun around, he extended his good leg and swept Mystro off her feet in one quick motion.

Mystro hit the floor hard and the wind was immediately knocked out of her, which caused her to drop the knife. The nigga watched as Mystro clawed for air on the floor with her weapon lying next to her head. He limped over toward her and picked up the knife with his right hand. Mystro looked up and had a clear view of his nut sack and ashy knees, standing over her head brandishing the knife. She just knew her life was over.

"Now, dyke, what the fuck you gonna do," the nigga said as he towered over top of Mystro while she continued to squirm on the floor trying to find oxygen.

He got on his knees and placed his left hand around Mystro's neck and squeezed tightly. He put the knife down near his knee on the floor. Then he spat in his empty right hand and grabbed his semi-erect dick and stroked it back to full attention.

"I'm 'bout to treat you like the bitch you really are," he said as he jerked his ten-inched dick over top of Mystro's face. She tried to free herself from his violent hold, but it was no use. This nigga was on some psychotic revenge shit and he had monkey strength.

"Yeah, dyke, I bet you ain't neva had no python 'bout to spit on that pretty face of yours huh," he teased as he continued to bring himself to the point of ejaculation.

Mystro had tears freely flowing from her eyes as she grabbed at his arm with all her might. Nothing she did seemed to work. He was too strong and too hateful.

"I don't give a fuck how much you try to be a nigga, mmmm, you can never do this, ahhhhhhhh," he yelled as he hunched his back and began convulsing out his orgasm. His thick, creamy nut shot out all over Mystro's braids and face. He continued to stroke and squeeze his dick until there was nothing left to escape it. To add insult to injury, he slapped the head of his dick onto Mystro's lips, taking one last shot at her. When he was sure he was finished, he freed his hand of his cock and picked the knife back up while he loosened his grip on Mystro's neck. She coughed hard, trying to breathe.

On the bed, Church began to stir from the temporary coma her man put her in with his fist. She tried to sit up but felt completely dizzy.

"Mystro, your services are no longer needed. You should've just stayed gone tonight. We took your saved up stash and was gonna roll out for good but now, I'm 'bout to take your life." He raised the knife to stab Mystro in the heart.

BOOM BOOM.

Two gunshots rang out as both bullets entered the nigga's head. His unresponsive body slumped onto Mystro, and the knife rolled out of his hand. She pushed him off of her and looked towards where the shots came from. Baby Dom and Native stood in the doorway of the bedroom. But it was Baby Dom, with wild eyes, who held the smoking gun that just ended the nigga's life.

"Noooooooooooooooooooooooooooo," Church screamed as she pulled her naked body off the bed and threw herself onto the floor on top of her dead nigga.

"Baby Dom, where the fuck you get that gun from," Native yelled. Baby Dom held the gun firmly, still aimed at the nigga's corpse.

"I grabbed it from under your couch when we went to the house to wait on Mystro to tell us what happened. I ain't want us to be naked out here. I knew we was prolly gonna walk into some shit," Baby Dom explained.

Mystro rolled onto her stomach, still coughing and tried to get on her knees to stand. Before completely getting up, she removed her T-shirt and wiped her face clean of the dead nigga's cum. Native ran over to help Mystro to her feet. She wanted her out of the line of fire, in case Baby Dom tried to shoot Church too.

Church held the nigga in her arms and rocked back and forth. This did nothing but set Mystro off even more.

"Nooooooo, baby, I'm so sorry, I should have gotten you out of this when you said something. It's my fault, baby, please come back to me." She cried as her tears fell onto his face.

Mystro could not believe what she saw. Fucking a nigga was one thing, but being in love with him was something altogether fucked up. Not being able to take anymore, she broke down. "Church, why would you do this shit to me, I thought you loved me." she cried out. Native held onto her friend tightly trying to support her weak body.

Church looked up at Mystro with a tear-soaked-red and swollen face, still holding onto the nigga's bloodied dead head. "Mystro, you are a fucking joke," she cried. "I never loved you, I only used you. Pussy on pussy ain't real. This is real," she continued referring to her dead nigga. "That bitch took away the true love of my life. I will kill you, dyke," she yelled shooting daggers at Baby Dom. "Do you hear me? I will murder your ass."

Baby Dom finally had enough of Church...she was done with her altogether. She raised the gun towards Church's head and prepared to take her life too. But Mystro, who also was sick of Church's shit, grabbed it out of her hand before she could fire.

Mystro turned to the love of her life and said, "Fuck you, Church. I hope you choke on that dead nigga's dick in hell, bitch." She squeezed the trigger and sent a hot one square into the middle of Church's black heart.

# EPILOGUE
## EIGHT MONTHS LATER

Mystro stood up in the crowded courtroom before Judge Tredall once again. This time she was the defendant in the double homicide of *Church Oliver* and *Grover Lawrence*. The night they were killed still played over in Mystro's mind repeatedly. After she took Church's life, she didn't shed another tear. It was as if the moment Church's soul left her body, a newfound strength entered into Mystro's.

"Before I allow the verdict to be read deciding your fate, Ms. Mason, I feel I need to address you personally," Judge Tredall said as he looked down from his seat on the bench and into Mystro's weary eyes. "Somehow I knew when you left my courtroom over a year ago, I would be seeing you again, although I hoped I didn't. I see you did not get treated for your obsessive ways and now, two lives have been taken," he continued to preach.

Mystro drifted off in her head. She was already on trial for both murders and did not feel like being chastised. Although she only took Church's life and not Grover's (the nigga), when she heard the sirens coming the night of the murders, she made Native take Baby Dom out of the apartment. She had to argue them both down before they finally left, because they were not trying to leave her behind.

Mystro's theory was simple. She killed Church in cold blood, and it made more sense for her to take the wrap of shooting the nigga too. After all, she did walk into her own apartment and found her girl-friend fucking another nigga. She figured instead of getting Baby Dom and Native involved any further in her own mess, she stood a better chance at taking the full brunt of the killings.

She felt Baby Dom already had a tough enough life and did not want her to waste the rest of it by being thrown into jail. Native finally understood Mystro's point and right before the law burst into Mystro's apartment, she snatched Baby Dom out of there. Now, it was her day in court to answer for that decision.

She felt even if she was found guilty, she might not get that much time. Her lawyer made great points during the trial of how Mystro went temporar-ily insane by walking into that scene. Then he ar-gued that after the initial stabbing, she had to defend herself against Grover's attack. He even brought up how Grover degraded Mystro by ejaculating all over her face while he held her down. She thought surely those points would play highly in her favor some-how.

As the judge continued on his pulpit grand-stand, Mystro looked around the courtroom. She saw the people she loved the most in the world sitting on her side, showing their love and support. Her cheerleading squad included Native and her mother, Margaret, Baby Dom, Brisa and Breezy. The saddest part about the outcome of this was that she might not have a chance to pursue a relationship with Breezy. There was no way she could ask her to wait for her if she was sentenced to jail, it wouldn't be fair. Besides, what if she never got out? She could not bring herself to put Breezy through that.

*'Maybe jail won't be so bad. I mean, I am gay, and I could prolly have any bitch in there I want. Shit, I can just go in, get on my prison throne and have 'em eating out my hands,'* Mystro thought. She looked at her supporters one last time before turning back around fully to face Reverend Deacon Judge Tredall and her verdict. But when she glanced over all of their faces, she noticed an awkward look in Baby Dom's eyes. She appeared to be staring off into another world, although she was looking directly at her.

The look concerned Mystro, but she needed to give the judge her full attention again. She shot Native an all knowing look and motioned her head towards Baby Dom.

Native picked up on her signal and looked at her.

"Baby Dom, you 'aight," Native whispered around her mother.

Baby Dom did not answer Native. She sat in silence and continued to rock back and forth while a single tear escaped each of her eyes.

"I'm sorry I had to preach to you, but no matter what the outcome of this trial is, I don't want it to be too late for you to change. Now, I will have the foreman read the verdict," Judge Tredall said as he turned to face the jury. "Madam Forman, can you please stand and read the verdict," he instructed. The middle aged black woman stood and opened the paper to announce Mystro's fate.

When out of the back of the courtroom, Baby Dom stood up and shouted, "You can't send her to jail for my crime. I killed the nigga, she didn't!"

# Drunk & Hot Girls

### The Complete Series

By

# LEGACY CARTER

CARTER PUBLICATIONS
PRESENTS

# Upscale KITTENS

A NOVEL

by Candee

CARTEL PUBLICATIONS
PRESENTS

**The Cartel Collection**
**Established in January 2008**
**We're growing stronger by the month!!!**
www.thecartelpublications.com

Cartel Publications Order Form
Inmates <u>ONLY</u> get novels for $10.00 per book!

| *Titles* | | *Fee* |
|---|---|---|
| Shyt List | _____ | $15.00 |
| Shyt List 2 | _____ | $15.00 |
| Pitbulls In A Skirt | _____ | $15.00 |
| Pitbulls In A Skirt 2 | _____ | $15.00 |
| Pitbulls In A Skirt 3 | _____ | $15.00 |
| Victoria's Secret | _____ | $15.00 |
| Poison | _____ | $15.00 |
| Poison 2 | _____ | $15.00 |
| Hell Razor Honeys | _____ | $15.00 |
| Hell Razor Honeys 2 | _____ | $15.00 |
| A Hustler's Son 2 | _____ | $15.00 |
| Black And Ugly As Ever | _____ | $15.00 |
| Year of The Crack Mom | _____ | $15.00 |
| The Face That Launched a Thousand Bullets | | |
| | _____ | $15.00 |
| The Unusual Suspects | _____ | $15.00 |
| Miss Wayne & The Queens of DC | | |
| | _____ | $15.00 |
| Year of The Crack Mom | _____ | $15.00 |
| Familia Divided | _____ | $15.00 |
| Shyt List III | _____ | $15.00 |
| Shyt List IV | _____ | $15.00 |
| Raunchy | _____ | $15.00 |
| Raunchy 2 | _____ | $15.00 |
| Raunchy 3 | _____ | $15.00 |
| Reversed | _____ | $15.00 |
| Quita's Daycare Center | _____ | $15.00 |
| Quita's Daycare Center 2 | _____ | $15.00 |
| Shyt List V | _____ | $15.00 |
| Deadheads | _____ | $15.00 |
| Pretty Kings | _____ | $15.00 |
| Drunk & Hot Girls | _____ | $15.00 |
| Hersband | _____ | $15.00 |
| Upscale Kittens | _____ | $15.00 |

**Please add** $4.00 **per book for shipping and handling.**
The Cartel Publications * P.O. Box 486 * Owings Mills * MD * 21117

Name: _____

Address: _____

City/State: _____

Contact # & Email: _____

**Please allow 5-7 business days for delivery. The Cartel is not**
**responsible for prison orders rejected.**

**<u>Personal Checks Are Not Accepted.</u>**

CPSIA information can be obtained
at www.ICGtesting.com
Printed in the USA
LVOW07s1652110417
530416LV00002B/239/P